CW00703882

The Problem with Sports

M.E. Clayton

Copyright © 2020 Monica Clayton

All rights reserved.

ISBN: 978-1-64970-431-3

DEDICATION

For my readers –
You guys really, really are the best!.

CONTENTS

ACKNOWLEDGMENTS

The first acknowledgment will always be my husband. There aren't enough words to express my gratitude for having this man in my life. There is a little bit of him in every hero I dream up, and I can't thank God enough for bringing him into my life. Thirty years, and still going strong!

Second, there's my family; my daughter, my son, my grandchildren, my sister, and my mother. Family is everything, and I have one of the best. They are truly the best cheerleaders I could ever ask for, and I never forget just how truly blessed I am to have them in my life.

And, of course, there's Kamala. This woman is not only my beta and idea guinea pig, but she's also one of my closest friends. She's been with me from the beginning of this journey, and we're going to ride this thing to the end. Kam's the encouragement that sparked it all, folks.

And, finally, I'd like to thank everyone who's purchased, read, reviewed, shared, and supported me and my writing. Thank you so much for helping make this dream a reality and a happy, fun one at that! I cannot say thank you enough.

PROLOGUE

"I…I understand if you need a moment," he said, his voice a practiced tone of compassion and patience.

Okay.

It could be worse, right?

Sure, they couldn't tell us what caused it, but did that really matter? What mattered was that it happened, and we needed to figure out how to move forward with it.

I looked over at Steven, and his head was bowed, his hands clasped before him. He looked like he'd gotten the worst news ever, but he hadn't.

We hadn't.

I looked back at Dr. Sorenson. "So, we just…have to monitor his activities, right?"

Dr. Sorenson smiled kindly. "Childhood interstitial lung disease varies from child to child," he said. "Though, it is a rare lung condition, chILD is not necessarily a debilitating diagnosis, Mrs. Hansen. The bronchoalveolar lavage showed no signs of lung injury, and that's a very good thing for Grant."

Steven remained silent, but I couldn't worry about him right now. I needed to understand what chILD meant for Grant. The poor thing was only five-years-old. "So…will he need inhalers and stuff?"

"It's a little more serious than that, but, yes, he'll need emergency inhalers. However, he may also need steroids, antimicrobial drug treatments, or bronchodilators should he have any breathing episodes," he explained. "It's quite possible he could be hospitalized and placed on a ventilator often, during his childhood, Mrs. Hansen."

I nodded nervously. "O…okay," I mumbled. "Then-"

"So, you're telling me that Grant's never going to be able to run around, jump on a trampoline, play sports, nothing?" Steven asked, finally speaking.

"Mr. Hansen, I understand-"

"Understand what, Doctor?" Steven rudely cut in. "Do you have a son you can't play with? Do you have a son who'll never play sports or live a normal life?"

Dr. Sorenson placed his arms on his desk and leaned forward. "There are many children who do not play sports, Mr. Hansen," he pointed out. "Lots of children are academically incl-"

"I didn't have a son just to watch him do math problems, Dr. Sorenson," Steven spat.

"Steven!" I cried, shocked at his level of negativity. Sure, Grant may struggle and there may be limitations placed on his life, but he wasn't dying. He didn't have cancer or only three weeks to live. He had a serious respiratory disease, but even then, it wasn't as bad as his condition *could* be. Didn't he just hear Dr. Sorenson say they'd found no lung damage yet.

Steven looked over at me "What, Andrea?" he barked. "He's basically telling us that Grant's going to be worthless. And-"

My eyes bugged and my blood fired hot. "Are you out of your mind?" I choked out. "He said no such thing, Ste-"

"He's not going to be able to do anything, Andre," he said, cutting me off. "What's a little boy if he can't run around with his friends or play any sports?"

This asshole.

"He's a little boy who is *alive*. And while he has a serious lung condition, it could be worse," I fired back. "Who gives a shit if Grant won't be able to play soccer as long as he's *alive!*"

"Mr. Hansen, Mrs. Hansen, I think it's best to hold off on this kind of discussion until you've both had time to work through your emotions, and maybe do a little more research on chILDs," Dr. Sorenson suggested. "Emotions can sometimes cause a situation to become more disruptive than it needs to be."

Steven stood up, and you could feel the fury coming off him in waves. "Well, since you just handed my wife the daughter she's always wanted, I'd say I'm probably the only one who needs to work through his emotions," he snarled, his words doing more damage than he could possibly understand.

"Do you really need to be such a bastard about this, Steven?" I snapped. He was sneering down at me as if this were all my fault somehow. "This isn't about you, Steven. This is about our son."

"A son who might as well be our daughter." I stood up, but before I could deck the sonofabitch, he added, "You better be ready to give me more children, Andrea, because I refuse to let this be it." He stormed out of Dr. Sorensen's office before I could respond.

But what would I say?

What could you say in response to something so devastatingly heartbreaking?

CHAPTER 1

Andrea – (Three Years Later) ~
There was more to life than sports.

There was art, academia, dance, Pokémon cards, all kinds of other things. But looking into the living room, Grant was sitting down, dressed from head to toe in Angels baseball garb, staring at the television. And if he wasn't watching baseball, he was watching football. And if he wasn't watching football, he was watching basketball. And if he wasn't watching basketball, he was watching hockey. And if he wasn't watching hockey…well, you get the picture.

Now, while the kid was sharp as a tack, his first love was sports. I was sure the only reason he excelled in school was because he wanted to be good at something, and since sports were out of the question, he tackled what he *could* do with all the determination of an eight-year-old boy.

And he seemed happy.

That was the most important thing about all this. Grant seemed happy, even if he couldn't play sports. He seemed happy to be able to admire his idols through the television. Maybe it was because he didn't know any different, so he didn't feel cheated, but whatever it was, I was grateful he seemed happy.

But even though I believed he was happy, I still made sure I did my best not to make his chILDs the focal point of his life. It was the reason I had moved into this condo after my divorce. There was no big backyard as a temptation to want to play outside, and the city park was damn near across town, so there wasn't that temptation, either. I knew he played a bit at school, but all the teachers knew about his condition, and Grant also took it seriously, even at the tender age of eight.

After Grant had been diagnosed with chILDs, things had gone downhill really quickly. While I had spent all my extra time researching chILDs and working with Dr. Sorenson on reasonable expectations for Grant, Steven had spiraled into self-depression. He had really believed that Grant had been lost to everything that made him a boy, and there'd been no talking him out of it. He couldn't get past this imagined life where he'd never get to play ball with his son, and I just couldn't understand how he just couldn't be happy that Grant was alive and the odds of him living a long life were extremely favorable.

Things had really gotten ugly when I had refused to have any more children with him. It wasn't that I had been opposed to having more kids, but I wasn't about to have them with someone who could so easily dismiss the one we'd already had. Besides, I'd had enough on my plate at the time with learning everything I could to help Grant lead as normal a life as possible.

A year later, Steven had walked out, and a quiet divorce had quickly followed. I had been heartbroken, but heartbroken for losing the man that I had married. I hadn't been heartbroken over losing the man he had become.

And now he picked up Grant every weekend and that was okay with me. I preferred having Grant with me as much as possible, so I could keep an eye on him. It wasn't that I didn't trust Steven to care for him properly, it was just that I was Grant's mother; that's it, that's all.

"You know, Mom," Grant called from the couch, "with all the trades happening, the season is in for a real shake up."

I walked further into the living room, then sat on the armrest of the couch. "Really?" As much as I couldn't care less about sports, it was hard not to know a thing or two with how much Grant followed them. You'd be amazed at the sports trivia I knew. "And which sport are we talking about?" He was watching baseball, but…

"Football, Mom," he said, his tone clearly indicating that I should know this.

I nodded, though he wasn't even looking my way. "Of course," I agreed. It was July, and I knew football preseason was going to start in August, and so even though he was watching baseball right now, that didn't mean anything.

"The draft wasn't too impressive, except for the running back from Oregon State, but I think I'm going to reserve any harsh judgements until after preseason." My lips curled in between my teeth, and I did my best not to laugh.

My kid was one of a kind.

"And Joel Schumacher's injury is career ending, poor guy," he said sympathetically.

"Joel Schumacher?"

Grant looked over at me-because commercial-and said, "The forward for the Oaks, Mom." *Ah, basketball.* "The poor guy isn't even two years into his contract."

Poor guy, indeed.

I knew I was going to lose him as soon as the commercials were over, so I said, "Hey, Grandma and Grandpa Miller sent me a text to tell you they'll be

Skype calling you later this evening." Grant smiled his excitement, but quickly focused his attention back on the game.

My parents, Donald and Mindy Miller, were retired and living on a small ranch in Montana. My father used to own a bar, which my brother, Justin, now owns and operates, and my mother used to be a city clerk. They had fallen in love with Montana a few years ago when they'd gone on vacation there, and when they decided to retire last year, that's where they had chosen to do it.

Justin was thirty-three, but he's been working at the bar since way before it was legal for him to be. He had begun working there in college, and two years into the collegiate lifestyle, he'd told Mom and Dad he wanted the bar. Even though Justin was older than me by three years, they had asked me how I had felt about it, and when I had made it clear that I'd had no interest in the bar, Dad had brought him onboard, and the rest was history.

And while I had met Steven in college and had gotten married early, Justin hadn't gotten married until about three years ago. I was happy for my brother, but it kind of sucked that our children were going to be so gapped in age. Grant was already eight, and while Justin and Nancy were pregnant right now, our kids were going to be damn near ten years apart. Justin might be three years older than me, but I was the one who had gotten an early start with marriage and children.

I headed into the kitchen to start dinner when my phone rang. I pulled it out of my pocket and smiled at the name flashing across the screen. Of course, I answered. "Hey."

"His name is Ted, he's a real estate developer, he's divorced with one daughter, and he's got two brothers." I closed my eyes, and almost thumped my head against the cabinet overhead.

Instead of giving myself brain damage, or a very big bruise, I let out a deep sigh. Rachel Filmore was my very best friend, and she has been for years. Unfortunately, she was very happily married and that made her think all women needed a man to be happy.

I didn't agree or disagree.

"Rachel," I bemoaned, "how many times do I have to tell you I'm not interested in blind dating?"

"It's been two years, Andie," she reminded me, but trust me, I didn't need reminding.

I grabbed a frying pan out of the cabinet. "I'm not opposed to meeting someone, Rach," I replied, feeling like we had this conversation at least once a week. "I just don't care for blind dating."

"Ugh," she sighed dramatically.

I really didn't have anything against dating, and I wasn't still hung up on Steven. Yeah, there were still these disheartening moments when the good memories would make random appearances in my mind, but I wasn't still in love with Steven. And while two years might seem like a long time, it really wasn't. Not when you had spent those two years picking up the pieces of your broken marriage, while at the same time learning everything you could about your child's illness. When Grant and I had moved into this place, almost a year ago, it was the first time since he'd been diagnosed with chILD that I'd felt like I could finally breathe. It had felt like things were finally beginning to settle, and it had felt…reassuring.

I wasn't sure if Steven was dating anyone right now or not, but I wouldn't be surprised if he were. He'd wanted more children, and I knew that no matter how many times he's apologized for the remark, that, deep down, he really wanted another son; one who wasn't broken. However, we didn't talk about our personal lives with one another. I dropped off Grant on Thursday evenings, and he dropped Grant off on Sunday evenings. That was it; no more, no less.

"Look, no more blind dates-"

"Don't you miss sex?" she asked, prioritizing.

Hell yeah, I missed sex.

"Of course," I admitted. "But not enough to sit through an uncomfortable dinner, forced conversation, fake interest…you name it. Not to mention, going through all that only to have the sex suck or be mediocre at best? No, thank you."

"Fine," Rachel relented. "Just promise me you'll make the effort to meet someone, okay?"

I was an independent editor and sometimes author, so there was really no need to leave my house, outside the basics of grocery shopping and whatnot. I understood where she was coming from. I *did* need to get out more.

"Deal," I agreed.

"You're lying," she accused.

I was.

CHAPTER 2

Nathan ~

There was more to life than sports.

There was family, friends, market shares, knitting, all kinds of other things. I've been retired from the MLB for only a few months, but you'd think that by now, I'd have gained a new hobby or something.

Right?

Don't get me wrong here. The decision to retire was the right one. I wasn't experiencing buyer's remorse or anything like that, not at all. It's just that baseball's been a part of my life since I was eight-years-old. I really didn't know anything else.

Growing up, my brothers, Gideon and Sayer, had no interest in sports as a career, so they'd been able to play a little of everything. And even as good at football as Sayer had been, he'd grown up to become a firefighter, and a damn good one. Gideon was a constructional engineer and was partners with our father in their business together. Sayer was the oldest at thirty-six, while Gideon was the middle child (and had the middle-child syndrome to prove it) at thirty-four, and I was the baby at thirty-three.

However, I had fallen in love with baseball the first time my father had signed me up for Little Tykes Baseball when I'd been six. My uncoordinated legs had run me around that diamond when I'd hit my first home run (the other six-year-old who'd been in right field had been chasing a butterfly), and when I had tripped on my shoelaces and face planted into home plate, that had been it for me.

I had fallen in love with baseball.

From there, my life had become nothing but school (because, legally, I had to), my brothers (because they lived with me), and baseball.

Well, and girls. Girls had been sprinkled in there because...well, they were girls.

And while my parents, Robert and Louise Hayes, had planned for college for all three of their children, landing a baseball scholarship to USC had certainly made things easier on them financially. And when I had made it to the pros, the first thing I'd done with my money was pay off their house and cars. I had wanted to do so much more with my money, but my parents weren't flashy people. They had taken the blessings of no longer having a house payment and car payments and had called it a day.

And when I had attempted to buy Sayer and Gideon their own homes, they had reminded me that they were men and could handle their own shit. At the time, I had tried not to take it personally, but I understood where they'd been coming from. I was their baby brother, and millionaire or not, they had wanted their successes to be their own.

So, since my family was self-sufficient, my money has been doing nothing but sitting in the bank, accumulating mad interest, and retirement at the age of thirty-three really hadn't been a problem.

Except, I was finding myself bored a lot these days.

The first couple of months of retirement had been spent moving into the top penthouse of my condominium building. But since I had a dick, it hadn't taken much to move in. I hadn't decorated or anything fancy like that. Despite having been a professional athlete, I'd never fallen into the money trap. Even my car wasn't anything upper-middle class American couldn't afford.

After getting situation in my new home, I had spent the following weeks loving on my mother. Louise Hayes had spent her entire life being a wife, mother, and homemaker, and she had loved every second of it. So, when I had finally flown the nest, she hadn't made a secret of how badly that had affected her. Unlike Sayer and Gideon, I was traveling all over the country, making conversation limited during the season, and Mom had played the guilt card like a professional. So, I had made sure to smother her with ten years of making up.

However, these days, she had Leta to smother, and so me, Gideon, and Sayer had a little more breathing room now. Leta was Sayer's stepdaughter. Sayer had married the love of his life in April, and Monroe had come with a fifteen-year-old daughter, who was about to turn sixteen (maybe I could buy her a car), but also a douchebag ex-husband. Oh, according to Sayer, Thomas (Monroe's ex) was doing a better job in the fatherhood department, but he still hated that Monroe had moved on with a younger guy, no matter that it had been Thomas who had divorced Monroe. We didn't like the man on principle, and until Sayer said differently that wasn't going to change.

The only problem with Sayer marrying Monroe was that it had put ideas in Mom's head. She had stink-eyed me and Gideon damn near throughout their entire wedding. Luckily, it had been a small and tasteful wedding, so Mom's crazy behavior hadn't ended up as an internet clip. But one thing was for sure; if I ever get married, Jake, Sayer's friend and fellow firefighter, was definitely planning my wedding.

And back to retirement being the right call, I knew I was fortunate to have retired when I did. No matter the sport, injury was a motherfucker. And if you were never outright injured, the wear and tear on your body was no joke. We got paid a shitload of money for what we did, but fans only got to see the excitement of the game. They weren't privy to the after-game moments where players were limping off the field, or in the locker rooms icing down their knees or shoulders. They weren't privy to the pre-game physical exams, where players were being shot full of cortisone injections or having their ribs taped up like goddamn mummies just to be able to play. Yeah, we were the ones who chose a career in sports, but that didn't mean we didn't earn our money.

I retired because I had wanted to enjoy the rest of my life. I hadn't wanted my golden years plagued with aches and pains beyond the normal ones that came with age. I hadn't wanted to undergo a million surgeries for my shoulder because I hadn't been smart enough not to stop when I should have had. And being the shortstop for the California Condors for the past ten years, my body had seriously started to feel those self-inflicted aches and pains.

As for women, luckily, I had fallen into that paranoid trap of not knowing if a woman liked me for me, or for my wallet. Now, don't get me wrong, because I've enjoyed my fair share of females throughout my career, but the obvious gold-diggers and team sluts had left a bad taste in my mouth. I hadn't been a saint by any means but witnessing the relentlessness of some of the fairer sex and watching fellow athletes cheat on their wives or get trapped by an unwanted pregnancy had gone a long way to making sure I paid special attention to where I stuck my dick.

And never without a condom.

Never.

My thoughts were cut short when my phone rang. Still appreciating the view my penthouse afforded me, I pulled it from my back pocket. Looking down, I grinned at the name flashing across the screen. "What's up?" I answered.

"I was going to text you, but I thought this warranted a phone call," Sayer replied, foregoing any sort of greeting.

"And why's that?"

"Leta's history class is covering political reporting and they have to do a project where they pretend to be investigative journalist," he explained. "I'm calling to warn you that Leta's going to call you and interview you for all the R-rated shit that goes down on the road with professional sports teams."

"What does playing sports have to do with investigative journalism for history?" No fucking way was I going to tell my niece the shit that goes on once the lights go off in the stadium.

"The students were able to choose their specific topic in history, and Leta chose sports and is doing a project on how sports have shaped history and how history has shaped sports," he replied. "I think Monroe may have influenced her choice." Sayer's wife was a sports freak. She didn't need to get fitted for a straitjacket just yet, but the woman loved her sports.

The traitor has also proclaimed the Dodgers as her favorite baseball team.

"And what's that got to do with threesomes after a game win?"

Sayer chuckled. "She's fifteen. She knows sex sells."

Fucking reality television.

"Well, thanks for the heads-up," I told him. "I'll be sure to make sure she keeps things G-rated."

"Thanks, man," he said. "Shit. I gotta go. They're looking for me."

"Where are you?"

"I'm hiding in the closet. Bye."

I stared at my phone and wondered how it came to be that my brother-*my oldest brother*-was scared of a fifteen-year-old girl.

My phone rang in my hand again, and this time it was Gideon. "What's up?"

"You have no excuses anymore," he barked into the phone. "Call your mother."

"I just talked to her yesterday, Gid," I barked back, swearing Mom pitted us against each other for entertainment purposes only.

"Then why did she just call me asking how you're doing?" he snarled, preferring to call me a liar instead of Mom.

"Because she's batshit crazy, Gid," I pointed out.

He hung up on me.

Goddamn it, Mom.

CHAPTER 3

Andrea ~

I wasn't sure how much longer I was going to be able to listen to this.

Now, don't get me wrong, because I loved our dinner chats and Grant really was the best dinner date ever, but the kid never stopped talking about sports.

And believe me, I've tried everything.

Every evening, during dinner, I asked him about school. I asked him about his friends. I asked him about his weekend plans with his father. I asked him about any new shows or movies that have caught his interest. I asked him about everything *but* sports.

However, the conversation always came back to trades, and injuries, and penalties, and corrupt umpires and referees, and even the up-and-coming college players.

I mean, I was all for having passion for something, but did it have to be *every* sport under the sun?

But I also wondered if it was because I always listened to him intently. Since Grant couldn't play sports, the only way he could enjoy them were through watching the games and knowing the players. Steven wasn't big on talking sports with Grant, and while I understood why I still hated it. Though Steven's come a long way since Grant was first diagnosed, Steven still had a tendency to make it all about himself at times.

"I don't see how he can continue to play, Mom," Grant said, and I thanked God he had enough manners in him to wait until he swallowed his food before dropping that sentence. "It's obvious the injury is more serious than they're letting on."

I took a drink of my water as I resigned myself to the topic of conversation. This was our last dinner together this week as I always dropped Grant off with Steven around five every Thursday. Though they weren't full days, the tradeoff allowed us both to have four days a week with Grant. There was no child support exchanged and I had chosen not to accept any alimony. Grant's treatments and preventative care was expensive, and it didn't benefit him if his father didn't have enough money to care for him properly should something happen. Steven was a real estate agent, and he did well for himself, but he wasn't rich. Plus, I did okay for myself. There had been no need to fight over money. Grant's health had been the priority for me back then and it still was.

"And who is this, honey?"

"Jansen Hillman," he answered. "He's the third baseman for the Detroit Irons, Mom." *Of course, he is.* "He got injured last year when Franco Marsalis slid into third and basically cleated the man out of a career."

I ate a couple of more bites of the enchilada casserole I had cooked up. "Well, it's a shame when someone gets injured."

Grant snorted. "It's a shame when they force these players to continue to honor their contract when they know it hurts them to play."

My heart warmed.

Grant loved his sports, and he was definitely a fanboy, but he wasn't so blinded by the fame and money that he stopped seeing athletes as human beings. He acted like he knew the players personally, and he cared about their health and well-being just as much as he cared about their stats.

"And that was the bad call last night," he continued. "I mean, how blind was that ump?"

I took another drink of my water. "You know, school's starting in a few weeks," I said, desperately trying to change the subject. "It's the third grade. Are you excited?"

Grant looked up at me, and it was times like these that my palm itched to slap the shit out of Steven. Grant was his exact replica with his dark blonde hair and green eyes. Looking at my son, I couldn't see any resemblance to me, whatsoever.

Even though I was blonde, too, I had more of a platinum color and my eyes were brown, instead of the classic blue usually associated with blondes. And where I was only five-foot-four, Steven was six-foot-one, and I was pretty sure Grant was going to inherit his height, too. The kid was growing like a weed.

Looking at my son, I knew he was going to grow up to be handsome, because for all of Steven's faults, the man was a good-looking male. He kept himself trim and fit and he'd been great in bed. I might not like the man much these days, but I wasn't going to create lies about him just because things had ended badly between us.

"I'm actually very excited," Grant replied, and I grinned at his grownup articulation. Sometimes it was hard to remember he was only eight.

"Really?"

Grant nodded. "Third grade is a whole new world, Mom," he said, grinning.

I smiled and went back to eating. But not two minutes later…

"Jansen Hillman's going to have to retire and that sucks," he said, returning to his favorite topic of sports. "And it's really a shame, Mom."

"It is?" I mean, I knew sports injuries were no joke, but they weren't the end of the world.

"Well, he's clearly the best third baseman to ever play for the Condors," he informed me. "As a matter of fact, he's probably their best player ever. And if he has to retire, then he's going to miss out on breaking all kinds of records." I sighed. "His batting average is .363, Mom. And he's hit a gazillion homers this season, so far," he replied with all the enthusiasm of a little boy. "His assists-"

"Okay, okay," I chuckled. "I get it. He's awesome." So, okay, this wasn't my favorite subject, but I loved seeing my son happy and excited.

Grant finished his forkful of food before speaking again. "He's more than awesome, Mom. Jansen really is the best player the Condors have ever had."

"Even better than the pitcher and catcher?" That was my only knowledgeable contribution to this conversation. Riveting, I know.

"Well, Marcos and Jennings are good, too, but..." Grant shook his little head. "…Jansen just has it all."

"Well, I'm sure whoever they find to replaced him will be just as talented," I assured him.

My kid scoffed.

"Yeah, like the shortstop they picked up to replace Nathan Hayes," he remarked all forlorn-like. "Granted, the guy will probably improve with experience, but one player can really change the entire dynamics of the team, Mom." *Dynamics?* The damn kid was talking as if he were grown.

"So, you…you liked this Nathan Hayes?"

Grant shrugged a shoulder. "He's no Jansen Hillman, but he was good, too. He's probably going to end up in the Hall of Fame someday."

"Well, then, surely, that means he was better than just good, right?"

"The guy just…he had a few more good years left, Mom," Grant said. "It was disappointing to see him bow out so soon."

"So, our favorite player is Jansen Hillman, then?"

Grant smiled. "He's our favorite player on the Condors," he corrected. The breeze kicked up a bit and a napkin flew into Grant's face, and we both laughed.

The condominium building that we lived in was nice beyond normal expectations. It had only ten floors, the top one being the only penthouse in the place, but each condo came with a balcony that Grant knew better than to play outside on. I came out here often, but Grant only came out here when we were having an outdoor dinner together. We lived on the ninth floor, so we were pretty high up. High up enough to make me uncomfortable if Grant was out here without me.

The condo was two-bedroom, one being a master bedroom with an en suite, one bathroom, a kitchen, living room, and a sitting room that I had converted into my office. The condos were nice, and they even came with their own washer and dryer. They cost a pretty penny, but after Steven and I had sold our house and had divided all our assets, I had been left with a decent down payment for the place. It wasn't a house in the suburbs with a yard and friendly neighbors, but it was our home. It was our home and Grant seemed happy here, and that was all that mattered.

"It's always nice when there's a breeze," Grant said, pulling the napkin from his face. "July is always so hot.

It wasn't often we ate out on the balcony during the hot summer months, but this week had cooled down significantly that tonight had been enjoyable enough to eat outside.

"Winter is still my favorite season," I replied, knowing we were on opposite sides on this topic.

"Well, there is football, hockey, and-"

"Yeah, yeah, yeah," I laughed. "I get it, son."

Grant grinned. "Since you've been a real trooper, we can watch Ridiculousness tonight," he graciously allowed.

"Deal," I agreed because I really did love me some Ridiculousness.

CHAPTER 4

Nathan ~

I wasn't sure how much longer I was going to be able to listen to this.

Jansen Hillman?

Seriously?

Now, don't get me wrong, because I absolutely adored the man. He was good people, and always the first to offer his help with anything. But the *best* player on the team? Sure, his average was impressive as hell, but it wasn't like he was playing a perfect game or hadn't fucked up a time or two.

And good?

Whoever the female was, she was right. You had to be better than good to even be *considered* for the Hall of Fame of any sport.

You didn't get in there by just being *good*.

And that was how I found myself standing in front of the door of apartment 903.

All the condos came with balconies, and I had been enjoying mine when the wind had picked up my neighbors' voices and had carried them upward, so that I could hear their conversation. Now, I didn't hang out on my balcony often because I had roof access to the pool and social amenities that had come with the penthouse purchase, but I had felt like enjoying the cool breeze that didn't happen often in July.

Then their voices had made it to my ears, and I couldn't just stand by and let this poor child be led astray. Clearly, his father was doing him a disservice by not setting him straight, so here I was.

About to set this kid straight.

I knocked on the door and waited.

And waited.

And waited.

I knocked again after about an hour (which was probably only really ten seconds), and *finally,* I could hear the lock disengage as someone was getting

15

ready to open the door.

I stood there, waiting patiently, and when the door swung open, I was greeted with a sight that threatened to turn me stupid.

She could only be topping at, maybe, five-foot-four, and she was petite as hell. Around thirty, or so, she had blonde hair and brown eyes, and she was just plain fucking stunning. She was dressed in a loose-fitting blue t-shirt, baggy ass jeans, and she was barefoot with toenails painted a pale yellow.

"May I help you?"

Fuck yeah, she may help me.

I mentally told my dick to shut the hell up and snapped myself out of my blonde-entranced stupor. "Do you have a kid in here?"

Her brows shot up and she started blinking rapidly. "Uhm…pardon?"

"A kid?" I repeated. "A very misinformed, misguided, confused child. Is he in there?"

"Excuse me?" she choked out.

"Mom, who is it?" came the misinformed, misguided, and confused voice behind her. Since 'Mom' was so much shorter than I was, it wasn't hard to see behind her. And there, stood a boy about eight-years-old and recognition immediately flashed in his eyes.

I invited myself in (by just brushing past 'Mom') and stood in front of the kid. "Jansen Hillman is *not* the best player on the Condors," I argued. "His average is great, don't get me wrong, but the *best?*"

The kid had the nerve not to take my word for it. "The only thing stopping him is his injury," he replied. "If he hadn't been injured, he'd be killing it."

"You're not even considering the PWA or PGP," I accused.

"The entire team's player win average had been affected with the recent *retirements,"* the little twerp fired back. "And Jansen's player game percentage has been compromised by his injury." He crossed his arms over his little chest. "I'd think you would know that."

The sound of the door shutting behind me reminded me that we weren't alone. And I was quickly reminded of it when the boy's mother came to stand in front of me. "Excuse me," she snapped. "Who in the hell are you? And what are you doing in my home?"

Who was I?

Was there no end to the insults?

"Mom, that's Nathan Hayes," her son said, cluing her in on who I was.

She turned back to face him. "Who?"

Christ on The Cross.

They'd *just* been talking about me.

The kid walked over to stand next to me. "Nathan Hayes, Mom," he repeated. "Remember? He just retired and is probably going to be in the Hall of Fame."

She shook her head, then looked up at me. "What are you doing here?"

she asked.

Was she for real?

"Doing what you so obviously are failing to do," I informed her. "Someone needs to set this young man straight about his baseball facts."

Her chocolate-colored eyes widened. *"Excuse me?"*

"I was out on my balcony, minding my own goddamn business, when I heard voices spreading fake news." I glared down at her son. "Specifically, a male voice."

"It's not fake news," he argued. "It's researched opinions."

I narrowed my blue eyes at the kid. "What's your name?"

"Grant," he supplied, narrowing his little green ones right back.

"And where is your father, Grant?" I asked before glaring back at his mother. *"Someone* needs to right this wrong."

"He's probably at home," he said. "But it doesn't matter. I'm not wrong."

"Oh, but you are," I informed the poor little confused dude.

"Opinions can't be wrong," he flung back. *"They're opinions."*

"Okay, that's enough," his mother said. She peered at me with those brown eyes of hers and you could see her visibly take a deep breath. "You need to leave, sir."

"Mom," her son rushed out, "you can't kick *Nathan Hayes* out of our house."

She turned to face him. "I'm pretty sure I can, Grant," she said, breaking the news to him. "I don't care who he is. He doesn't just get to come into our house and...and..." She looked at a loss. "...challenge you on your right to have your own opinions."

"I'm not challenging his opinions," I lied. "I'm trying to set the kid straight since you obviously don't care enough to do it."

Her brown eyes narrowed at me, the threat in them clear. "It's *just* sports," she spat. "We're not talking about the fate of humanity here."

Did she just...?

Did she just say...?

Just sports?

I pointed a finger at her. "I'm going to go," I announced. "But only because I can't even look at you right now. *Just sports?* Really?"

"He's got a point, Mom," Grant said, the precious, adorable child that he was.

"Oh, sweet Heaven," she mumbled.

"I'm going to go," I repeated. "But I'll be back." I pointed towards Grant. "I am not going to just stand by and let you...leave him to his own devices."

"Are you insane?" she asked.

I ignored her uncalled-for question and looked back at Grant. "This weekend-"

"I'll be with my dad this weekend," he said, cutting me off. "I go with my dad on Thursdays and don't come back until Sunday. When I'm going to school, I go with him on Fridays and come back on Sundays."

"So, he's the one who takes you to games?" I asked.

Grant shook his head. "No," he replied. "We've never been to any games."

"Baseball games?"

He shook his head again. "No. No games. For any sport."

I glared back at his mother. "I just can't with you right now," I growled at her before walking out of their condo, slamming the door behind me.

What kind of fucking father didn't take his kid to sports games? Especially, a kid who was so obviously into sports. I couldn't even throw the kid off with the PWA and PGP references.

I clearly needed to get to the bottom of this, and I was not going to let his hot as fuck mother distract me from what was important here.

No matter how hot she was.

No. Matter. How. Hot. She. Was.

CHAPTER 5

Andrea ~

I couldn't believe I was having this conversation.

I mean, I've had a lot of strange conversation with Rachel over the years, but this had to be the strangest by far.

"So...then...he just left?" she asked just as confused as I had been when Nathan Hayes had stormed out of my condo last night.

After *the* Nathan Hayes had slammed the door behind him last night, Grant had been appalled-*absolutely appalled*-that I had just let him leave like that. When I had broken it to Grant that I hadn't *let* Nathan do anything, he had pointed out how I'd failed to offer the man any refreshments, enticing him to stay. But before I could defend myself, he had gone full-blown fanboy on me and had lost his mind over knowing that Nathan Hayes lived right above our condo.

And what a Nathan Hayes he was.

I was only five-foot-four, but that didn't mean I couldn't tell that he was at least foot taller than me, and he wasn't lanky tall, either. The man was a mountain of muscles and masculinity with a dark brown hair and bright blue eyes combo. His face was chiseled perfection, and he looked like he belonged on a box of Wheaties.

The man was simply gorgeous all over.

"Yeah," I replied. "It was...weird."

Rachel chuckled. "I still don't understand how you didn't know who he was."

"I don't follow baseball, Rach," I reminded her.

"You don't need to follow baseball to know who Nathan Hayes is, Andie," she laughed. "Everyone who's ever lived in this town knows who Nathan Hayes is. He's a local boy who made it to the pros. There have been a million interviews with him about his life, family, and career."

"I guess I never paid attention," I muttered.

"Jesus, Andie. The man is a legend," she went on to inform me. "His parents live here and one of his brothers is even a firefighter for Silias County. The other one is an engineer or something."

"I really have no idea what you're talking about," I told her.

"That's the problem," she joked. "The man just retired and the news about it was *everywhere*. Which goes to prove that you need to get the hell out of your house, Andie."

"Rach-"

"Or better yet, you know where the man lives," she kept right on rambling. "Make your way up to his door with some sexy lingerie and get laid, girl."

I choked out a laugh. "Rachel, if what all you're saying is true, the man is a famous athlete," I pointed out. "I'm sure he's covered in that department."

"The stuff I am saying *is* true," she insisted. "But what does that matter? You're sexy as hell, Andie. He'd be crazy to turn you down."

Sometimes I wondered if she listened to the things that came out of her mouth. It was a wonder Charlie didn't muzzle the woman. Of course, Charlie claims to have fallen in love with Rachel at first sight, so there was very little she could do wrong in his eyes. They'd met their sophomore year at Columbia when Rachel had stormed into the student advisory office to dispute her dorm assignment and Charlie had been the poor bastard who had been working the student advisory. She had called him an idiot and he had chased her for three months before she had finally agreed to a date.

Over ten years later, he still adored the hell out of her.

"Rachel," I said, sighing, "I am thirty-years-old, divorced, and have a kid who left plenty of proof of his existence on my body. I seriously doubt Nathan Hayes, retired professional baseball player, is going to even look at me as an option."

"And-"

"And before you scold me because you think I'm being too hard on myself, I'm not," I told her. "I'm stating simple facts, Rach. That man can get any woman he wants. He doesn't need to resort to single mothers who don't know anything about sports."

"How do you know he doesn't want something different?" she challenged.

"Different from perfection?" I asked, the sarcasm obvious.

"Don't judge a man you know nothing about, Andrea," she chided.

"I'm not judging him, Rachel," I denied. "But I know you know what the man looks like."

"Okay, so, yeah, maybe he looks like he should live on Mount Olympus, but-"

"*Maybe?*"

She sighed. "Fine," she exhaled dramatically. "He's beyond perfect and can get any woman he wants. But still, that doesn't mean you can't be that woman."

Rachel was forgetting one very real and serious concern. "Rach," I said sternly, "the man barged into my home and started arguing with Grant over baseball opinions. He's clearly taken one too many balls to the head."

"Why does he have to be crazy?" she countered. "Why can't he just be passionate about the subject? He *is* a retired baseball player after all."

"Did you miss the part where he knocked on a stranger's door to challenge an eight-year-old?" I reminded her. "He's clearly crazy."

"Oh, please," she scoffed. "If you had even a tiny inkling that he was dangerous or really crazy, you would have called the police, Andie. That man is not crazy."

While she did have a valid point, I still couldn't dismiss how he had barged into my home, like a lunatic, to argue baseball with a child. However, he hadn't come across mean or threatening. He had actually seemed upset that Grant hadn't chosen him as the best Condors player ever.

I shook my head. Maybe retirement was making him loopy.

And then a thought occurred to me. "Rachel, you can't tell anyone Nathan's my neighbor," I blurted out. "If it gets out that he lives here this place will start crawling with tabloid vultures and gold-diggers."

"Firstly, I know better," she retorted. "And secondly, I doubt he would have bought that penthouse if he hadn't believed it was safe and private."

"Well, if everyone knows he retired and has come back home, then–"

"Andie, he'd have the problem of being famous, no matter where he lived," she pointed out. "I'm sure he knows what he's doing."

The entire thing was…weird.

And not that there was a chance he'd ever be interested in me, but I couldn't deny it was a nice fantasy to indulge in. If I was going to fling the chastity belt off, then who better with than someone who was built like Nathan Hayes? One look at the man and how could you not think about wall sex?

"Well, even if I were interested–"

"You have a pulse. I don't see why you wouldn't be," she interrupted.

"–I seriously doubt Nathan Hayes is the guy to take the training wheels off with," I retorted. "I need a nice, boring, mild-mannered CPA or something to practice with first."

Silence.

Complete silence.

"Rach?"

"Are you telling me that after over two years without sex you want your first time to be with someone who's going to insist on keeping his socks on?" she asked incredulously. "You want your first time to be *boring?*"

"Not boring," I denied. "Just…something tells me sex with Nathan Hayes would be explosive, and that would suck–"

"*What?*"

"All I'm saying is it would be a tough act to follow," I clarified. "The last thing I want to do is have mind-blowing sex, then have to make do with average afterwards."

Rachel snickered. "So, you're saying Nathan Hayes would ruin you for all other men, huh?"

"Are you saying he wouldn't?" I harrumphed.

"Good point," she finally conceded.

"Okay. As fun as it's been fun discussing my dry spell and how Nathan Hayes has to be at least a little bit crazy, I gotta go," I told her. "I have to drop Grant off in a couple of hours, and I need to get my lovin' in before he abandons me for three days."

"You really need a man," Rachel advised before just hanging up. I let out a laugh as I placed my phone on the kitchen counter.

For all of Rachel's good intentions, starting something with Nathan Hayes was as likely as me starting to play for the Condors.

A professional baseball player?

Really?

CHAPTER 6

Nathan ~

I couldn't believe I was having this conversation. But then who else would I be talking to about this?

One of the problems with being famous was that you never knew who was willing to sell you out for a dollar. Even as much as I trusted my best friend, Sergio Hernandez, a fellow Condor, I still couldn't guarantee that he'd never sell me out if the price were right.

There were only four people on the planet I trusted completely: Mom, Dad, Sayer, and Gideon. And while I also trusted Monroe and Leta, knowing Sayer the way I did there was always a good chance he could piss Monroe off to the point where she'd burn my entire family to the grown, so there was that.

So, sitting in my penthouse, I was telling my brothers all about my neighbor downstairs and the disservice she was doing her son by letting him walk around with wild ideas and misinformed opinions.

"So...you just barged into their home and went toe-to-toe with an eight-year-old?" Gideon asked, missing the point entirely.

"Jansen Hillman is not the best player on the team, Gid," I informed him. "He's good, don't get me wrong, but the best?"

"Maybe we're being a bit sensitive that the kid called you good instead of great?" Sayer suggested. He was on his three days off rotation, and usually he spent every free second that he had with his wife and stepdaughter, but they were having a spa day with Mom and no one was stupid enough to deny Mom anything.

Dad would slaughter us all.

"But he did say you'd end up in the Hall of Fame," Gideon pointed out.

"His name is Grant, and I'm not being sensitive," I denied.

My brothers shared a look before Sayer cleared his throat. "You barged into their home, Nate," he reiterated. "You're being sensitive, or you've turned crazy. Either way, you can't be just barging into people's homes and arguing their opinions." He popped a grape into his mouth as I narrowed my eyes at him.

Between the three of us, there was barely anything left on the fruit platter that Gideon had brought over. When Mom found out we were all getting together at my house, she had made a healthy fruit platter and had bullied Gideon into bringing it with him. Never mind that I had food in my house and that this wasn't a tea party. Gid and Say were my brothers, for fuck's sake. They could help themselves to my refrigerator if they were hungry. I didn't need to entertain these two assholes.

I looked at my oldest brother. "So, what? I'm just supposed to stand aside and let them raise him to be a psychopath?" I asked, shocked that he would suggest such a thing. "I mean, while there's no helping your Dodger-loving wife, there's still hope for Grant."

"You don't think the boy's parents might take exception to you kidnapping him and raising him as your own?" Gideon scowled.

"I'm not trying to kidnap him, Gid," I corrected. "I'm just trying to put the kid back on the right track."

"He debated stats with you, Nate," Sayer said after popping another grape in his mouth and swallowing. "I think the kid is already on the right track."

"I'm surprised his mother didn't call the cops on you," Gideon added, again, missing the entire point of me calling them over here. They were supposed to support me and my ideas, damnit. Not root for the enemy.

"So, what is your plan, exactly?" Sayer asked, sounding supportive but wary.

"Well, he spends his weekends with his dad, so that only leaves me the weekdays to bring him back over from the dark side," I replied. "Not sure what his mother does for a living, but surely, she wouldn't be opposed to free babysitting, right?"

Gideon shook his head. "This sounds like such a bad idea," he mumbled.

"It's a great idea," I argued. "She gets free daycare, and the kid starts out on the path of life the right way."

"And the dad has no say?" Sayer asked, but only because he was tied up with a douchebag of an ex-husband.

"If he wanted a say in what his son did during the weekdays, then he shouldn't be a weekend-only father," I pointed out. Granted, I had no idea why Grant's parents were divorced, or even if they were, but it was clear they weren't one big happy family if they were sharing custody.

"C'mon, Nate," Gideon remarked. "You have no idea what their family dynamic is. Don't bite off more than you can chew, dude."

I scoffed like a locker room bully. "Why? What's he going to do? Beat me up?" I was a professional athlete, and six-foot-four of pure muscle. Even though I retired a few months ago, that didn't mean I had let myself go. I had a personal home gym and I used it daily.

"So, that's your plan?" Sayer asked. "You're going to beat up his father and kidnap him from his mother?"

"Best plan you've ever had," Gideon deadpanned.

"You guys have a better one," I challenged.

"Yeah," Gideon scoffed. "Mind your own goddamn business and let the poor kid like who he likes."

I narrowed my eyes at him. "How about you go eat a dick," I fired back.

"Are you even sure Grant would be onboard with you beating up his dad and kidnapping him from his mother?" Sayer asked. "I mean, that's something to consider, Nate."

This conversation was ridiculous.

"You assholes are the ones who said I needed to find something productive to do in my retired years," I pointed out.

Gideon's blue eyes that matched all the Hayes men widened. "Not assault and kidnapping, Nate."

"Maybe he won't have to resort to kidnapping," Sayer chimed in. "You *are* Nathan Hayes. Bat them baby blues at her and she'll probably come around." Sayer grinned. "Bat them at the dad, too. That might work."

I popped an apple slice in my mouth, buying some time before telling these two jerkfaces the truth. After making sure I wouldn't be talking with my mouth full, I said, "I'm pretty sure she's immune to the baby blues."

Both assholes smirked.

"If my looks were a plus in this situation, she wouldn't have thrown me out of her house last night," I admitted.

"Wait." Gideon's brows drew downward. "I thought you said you stormed out of there."

"Semantics."

"Yeah," Sayer replied dryly. "Because leaving on your own and getting thrown out are basically the same thing."

"Is she hot?" Gideon asked, a smirk on his face.

"She might be," I hedged, but there was no 'might be' about it. At first glance, I had thought she was stunning, but when she had gotten in my face and fought for her son, she had transformed into radiant. Her blonde hair thrown up in a bun, no makeup on her face, and barefoot, she was one of the hottest women I have ever seen, and I've seen some hot fucking women in my lifetime.

However, those women always had the same thing in common. Their hair was always perfect, their makeup always looked professional, and their outfits left little or nothing to the imagination.

Grant's mother was a stunner without all that shit.

Gideon laughed. "Now it all makes sense," he smirked.

"Fuck you, dude," I tossed back. "Her looks have nothing to do with this."

Sayer looked over at Gid. "You're forgetting he stormed down there even before he knew what the mother looked like."

"Thank you, Say," I said, happy to have at least one brother's support.

"The kidnapping was probably already a given," Sayer continued. "But I'm betting kicking the ex-husband's ass came after he saw what she looked like."

"Get out of my house."

"Gladly," Gideon replied. "I have better shit to do than plan assault and kidnapping with you two fucks."

"Like what?" Sayer asked.

"Yeah, like what?" I echoed because we both knew Gideon didn't have anything better to do. It was past working hours and that's all the man did. He worked.

"Like not catch any felonies," he retorted, and then walked out of my house, but not before snatching up the rest of Mom's fruit platter and taking it with him.

The jackass.

CHAPTER 7

Andrea ~

This crap did not make any sense.

Like, none, *at all.*

When I had dropped Grant off with Steven earlier, it was the first time since our divorced that Grant seemed reluctant to spend the weekend with his father, but I suspected that had to do with knowing that Nathan Hayes was his upstairs neighbor.

All day, Grant had been asking me questions that I didn't have the answers to. He had asked if I thought Nathan was mad at him. He had asked if I thought Nathan would come back and visit us. He had asked if I thought Nathan would go back to playing baseball. He had been all about Nathan Hayes, but the one thing that I'd been happy about? While Grant had relented and had admitted to Nathan Hayes being better than just good, he hadn't changed his stance on Jansen Hillman being his favorite player. And he hadn't switched teams. His favorite baseball team was still the Angels. There were a few California baseball teams to choose from, and when sports had started to matter to Grant, he had chosen the Angels, and has stuck with them this entire time. All his favorite teams were California teams. The kid was loyal, if nothing else.

However, that wasn't what I was feeling flummoxed over. No. I was feeling out of sorts and confused as all hell because I was currently standing in my doorway, the door wide open, staring at Nathan Hayes in the flesh. And I wasn't going to lie, speech was a struggle when face-to-face with a man as sexy as Nathan Hayes was. Without the shock of last night's visit and Grant here to take up his attentions, maintaining eye contact with the god was a struggle.

"May I help you?"

"May I come in?"

Hell no.

"Oh, we're asking this time?" I couldn't help myself. Baseball god or not, the man shouldn't just be barging into people's homes.

He cocked a brow.

I let out a deep sigh. "Grant's not here," I told him. "He's with his father until Sunday evening."

"I know," he replied. "He explained his schedule to me yesterday. Remember?"

"Then why are you here?" I asked, confused by a whole lot of things.

"May I come in?" he asked again, and while I thought it was a bad idea, I pulled the door open to let him inside.

"Would you like something to drink?" Though this seemed like a bad idea, I wasn't going to be rude or a jerk. He could have a very legitimate reason for being here. We were neighbors after all.

"No, thank you," he replied as he looked around, taking in my home. I was positive it wasn't as lavish as his penthouse must be, but I loved it here.

"Then what can I help you with, Mr. Hayes?"

He crossed his massive arms over his chest as he stood in my living room and those startling blue eyes of his narrowed a bit. "What's the deal with you guys never taking him to a ballgame?"

"Get out of my house," I replied, quickly and surely.

"Excuse me?"

"I know you're a baseball god and all, and you're probably used to people tripping over themselves to please you, but I really don't care who you are," I told him. "You don't get to come into my house and start demanding answers about my son and how he's being raised."

His arms fell to his sides and his eyes narrowed a bit more. "Is there some religious reason Grant's never been to a ballgame before?" Nathan asked, ignoring my entire statement.

I planted my hands on my hips. "Explain to me how this is any of your business?"

"Even if his views are skewed, it's obvious he loves sports," he replied. "Why wouldn't taking him to a game be a birthday present or something?"

"*Again,* how is this any of your business?" I wasn't sure what this lunatic was about, but I hated the way he made it seem as if Steven and I were horrible parents because we didn't take our son to ballgames.

And while I had nothing against taking Grant to some games, Steven felt strongly against it and it wasn't worth the fight. Especially, when I knew, deep down, Steven was doing it for the same reason I bought a condo and not a house with a yard. We didn't want to rub Grant's limitations in his face.

"It's not, if you want to argue legalities and morality, but I'm not here to do that." My brows shot up. "I'm here because it pains me to know that kid has never been to a game."

I rolled my eyes. "You'll get over it."

Nathan shook his head. "No, I really don't think I will," he countered.

"Can I take him to a game or not?"

This man really was a stone-cold psychopath.

"No," I said, dragging the word out, so he'd understand what I was saying. "Why not?" he asked like a petulant child.

"Because I don't know you," I reminded him. "You're out of your mind if you think I'm just going to let some stranger take my child *anywhere.*"

He looked genuinely perplexed when he said, "But I'm Nathan Hayes." "So?"

His mouth opened and closed like he was at a loss for words. And he probably was. He probably believed his superstar status gave him a free pass or something. Now, did I think Nathan Hayes would kidnap Grant? Probably not. But that was a *probably* not, not a concrete no.

After a couple of awkward minutes, he finally spoke. "Why hasn't he ever been to a game?"

I wasn't sure what it was, but something in Nathan's voice moved me. He was asking me because he genuinely wanted to know and not in some judgmental way. Grant's love for sports was obvious, and Nathan was genuinely curious.

"Would you like to sit down?" I asked, extending an olive branch.

He gave me a terse nod. "Thank you, yes," he replied before making his way to the couch.

"Drink?"

I could hear his low chuckle. "Yes, please. Water, if you have it."

I went and grabbed two waters, then made my way to the couch. I sat down but made sure to sit far enough away that there was an entire cushion between us.

Handing him his water, I fiddled with the one in my hand. Not many people knew about Grant's condition and it wasn't something I often talked about. However, with Nathan being who he was, plus our upstairs neighbor, it was probably a good idea to let him know, so that he didn't fill Grant's head with any harebrained ideas.

"Do you know what interstitial lung disease is?" Nathan shook his head. "It's a lung disease that affects children, teens, and young adults."

"Okay."

"The best way I can describe it as is a severe case of asthma that sometimes comes with actual lung damage," I explained. "Grant has to be monitored and needs a bronchoalveolar lavage performed every two years to monitor for damage, and we've been lucky that he doesn't have any. Or at least, he hasn't had any since he was diagnosed three years ago."

"So, he doesn't play *any* sports?"

I shook my head. "No, he doesn't," I confirmed, a pang in my chest. "While chILD, that's what it's referred to, affects children differently, Grant doesn't have any lung damage right now. So, Steven and I decided to do all we can to make sure no damage develops, and part of that is not playing sports."

Nathan looked upset, and it touched me deep inside. "And...he's not sad about that?"

"If he is, he's never said anything about it," I told him. "When he's not at school or playing with his friends, he's consuming sports, and not just baseball. He loves all sports. Football being his favorites. He's-"

Nathan put his hand up to stop me. "Football? Seriously?" he asked, visibly upset for a different reason now. "Have you people no consideration for me at all?"

"Uh..."

"First, I'm not his favorite Condor player. Second, I'm just *good*, even though I am bound for the Hall of Fame. Finally, baseball isn't even his favorite sport? What the fuck?"

It was everything I could do to keep my laugh in.

This man was serious.

"Is that really the point right now?" I asked, trying my damnedest not to laugh.

Nathan narrowed his eyes at me again-something I was noticing he did often-and asked, "Because those aren't important concerns?"

Good Lord, Nathan Hayes really was crazy.

CHAPTER 8

Nathan ~

This crap did not make any sense.

Like, none, *at all.*

Even though I knew nothing about chILD, I understood why Grant might not be able to play sports. Medical reasons. Totally legit. But to never have taken him to a game? That was just plain fucking crazy.

"You know," she drawled out slowly as if she were addressing a crazy person, "there are children, all over the world, who claim you as their favorite Condor player, and claim the Condors as their favorite team, right? It's okay if Grant doesn't think-"

"What's your name?" I asked, cutting off whatever crap she was about to spew, justifying Grant's wrong ways.

"Andrea Miller," she replied. "But most people call me Andie."

"Does Grant share your same last name?" I was being super nosey and overstepping, but I needed to know if assault and kidnapping were really on the menu.

She cocked a brow. "You do realize you're being extremely intrusive, right?"

I waved away her very valid point because I needed to know what I was up against. "Look, Andrea, Grant and I are going to become the best of friends, so I suggest you make this relationship as painless as possible."

"What relationship?" she asked cautiously.

"Ours." Has the woman not been paying attention?

"Uhm, excuse me?"

I let out a deep breath, and quite frankly, the woman was frustrating. Hot as molten lava, but still frustrating.

"Did you, or did you not, state earlier that you would never let your son go to a game with a stranger?" She just blinked at me, so I took that as my cue to continue. "So, the obvious solution to that is for us to become friends, right?"

She curled her lips in between her teeth, then gnawed on them a bit. After a few seconds, she asked, "So, you want to be friends with me, so that you can take Grant to a game? Is that it?"

Beautiful, but a bit slow on the uptake. "How else am I going to be able to take him?"

She shook her pretty little head before finally answering, "Grant's last name is Hansen."

"So, you're divorced?" And of course, I was asking strictly for Grant's sake. The fact that she was beautiful with a smokin' body had nothing to do with it.

"Two years," she replied. "But…I'm only telling you this, so that you understand that Grant has a father. And Steven feels very strongly about Grant going to ballgames."

Steven sounded like an asshole.

But I wasn't going to tell her that.

Instead, I asked, "Why?"

She let out a tired sigh, and her hands started tearing at the label on her water. "Grant will never be a professional baseball star, Nathan," she said. "He'll never play soccer, or football, or hockey, or anything. It…it seems cruel to take him around something he loves so much, knowing he'll never get to experience any of it."

I thought about that.

After a few minutes of uncomfortable silence, I asked, "What do you think is worse, taking a boy to a ballgame, even though he knows he can't play, or putting a kid into sports all his life, even knowing that he'll probably never play professionally?"

"What?"

I wasn't taking her concerns lightly. Even with all the new gender-neutral expectations these days, there were still a lot of people who expected girls to play with dolls and boys to play sports. But no matter your views, a child not being able to play sports, or games, or even just exercise for health reasons was sad. So, I understood not wanting to put alcohol in front of a recovering alcoholic, but then why let him watch sports? Why let him become obsessed them at all? Or, maybe, that was their way of giving him a safe taste of sports. I wasn't sure, but in my opinion, letting a kid go to a game, even though he'll never play it, was less cruel than making a kid play sports, trying to force the talent, only to come up empty in the end. It took more than talent to hit the pros.

"Grant already knows he can't play sports, so he's untainted by the lights and glamour. He enjoys sports for what they are, not for the celebrity they've become. He's a true sports fan, unlike a lot of kids who are forced into sports by their parents, fame and money being the motivator. And most of them never succeed, so talk about crushing a dream," I explained. "I think you're doing a disservice by not taking Grant to any games."

She stared at me a bit before saying, "Huh." Andie started chewing on her lower lip. "I...I never thought of it that way," she admitted.

"Look, I'm not trying to...downplay your concerns," I told her. "I have no experience with chILD, outside of what you just told me. But...there are thousand kids in those stands who can't play sports but still love to go to the games, and they have a great time." Then a thought occurred to me. "Have you guys even asked Grant how he feels about going to a live game?"

Her cheeks turn a slight shade of pink. Andie shook her head. "No," she admitted. "It was a decision Steven and I agreed upon when he'd been diagnosed, and we sort of just left it at that."

I nodded my head and thought about everything we'd just discussed. After a few seconds I said, "Okay, there's a lot to unpack here, but we're going to start with our relationship, bec-"

"Our relationship?" Her voice sounded wary again.

"Yes, our relationship," I repeated. "We have to become friends or none of this will work."

She inclined her head a bit. "None of *what* will work?"

"Jesus, woman," I breathed out. "Pay attention, will you?"

Her brows shot up. "Oh, trust me, I'm trying. However, you're making no sense."

I narrowed my eyes at her lie. "If we don't become friends, then how else am I supposed to steer Grant back on the right path?"

She narrowed her brown eyes right back. "He's not on the *wrong* path," she argued.

I cocked my head. "His favorite sport is football," I began, ticking off Grant's list of offenses with my fingers. "He can't decide if hockey or baseball is his second. And when it comes to baseball, his favorite team is the Angels, *and* he thinks Hillman is the best Condors player. Not to mention, he called me *good*, even though I'm slated for the Hall of Fame." I put my hand back down, my ticks finished. "There's *a lot* wrong with all of that."

"You do know this is America, right?" she remarked like a smartass. "In this country, people are entitled to their own opinions."

"People have the right to their own opinions all over the world," I corrected her.

"Yeah, but in America you don't get stoned for them," she countered.

"That's debatable," I replied. I was raised by a meddling mother. If Sayer, Gideon, or I ever dared to tell Mom our opinions on her meddling ways, we'd be worse than stoned. There was a good chance no one would ever see any of us alive ever again.

"Look, your mental illness aside, you made a valid point about the live games," she said. "I'll talk to Steven about it and see what he says."

"And if he says no?" Admittedly, I knew nothing about the guy, but he sounded like a dick so far. I also didn't like how cozy she seemed with him. Sure, it was absolutely none of my business, but a few of my body parts were eager to become friends with this woman, and so I needed to know what I was dealing with here.

Andie shook her head. "Then we'll talk about it some more," she replied. "Believe it or not, Grant really is our number one priority."

"Why wouldn't I believe it?"

She shrugged. "Lots of divorced couples never make it past the hurts and/or betrayals to do what's best for the children. That's not me and Steven."

I didn't know what to say to that. I didn't want to sound like a dick, but it seemed that if Grant was their number one priority, they never would've gotten divorced. Of course, I didn't know the details, so what did I know? I just knew I didn't like hearing her speak like they were a team.

Fuck, I needed to get a grip.

I stood up, ready to leave. "Okay, so talk to Steven, and then we can get to work on helping Grant see the light."

Andie stood when I did, and I could tell she was trying not to laugh again. "You do know you're going to fail, right?" she asked. "Grant's loyalty is solid."

"We'll see about that."

CHAPTER 9

Andrea ~

I had expected some friction, but not a full-blown argument.

After Nathan had left my condo Thursday evening, I had thought a lot about what he had said. Grant was very aware of his lung disease. He knew there were restrictions with his physical activity. He knew there was little to no chance that he'd ever be a sports celebrity. So, would taking him to a game really be so traumatic for him? And how was that any different from him watching the games on television? It was worth talking to Steven about because Nathan really seemed determined to befriend Grant.

Nathan had also made it crystal clear that his only interest in our household was Grant. After we had spoken some more about Grant's condition and I had filled him in on everything I knew about chILD, he had asked if he could stop by on Monday to see Grant and when I had assured him that it would be okay, he had politely excused himself.

Now, granted, I knew the odds of Grant playing professional soccer were a lot higher than Nathan Hayes being interested in me, but it had been fun to fantasize about the idea. While everything I had said to Rachel was true, a girl couldn't look at Nathan Hayes and not think things.

Well, at least, this girl.

So, when Steven had dropped Grant off a half hour ago, I had asked him if he could stay, so we could talk. He agreed, and since I didn't want Grant overhearing us, we had gone out to the balcony. However, this time, I made sure to listen for any noises coming from the balcony above us.

But before I could launch into my spiel, Steven had assured me that he already knew Nathan Hayes was living in the penthouse on the top floor. Apparently, Grant hadn't shut up about meeting Nathan all weekend.

Steven had given me the opening I needed, but I quickly found out that hadn't necessarily been a good thing.

Our argument kind of confirmed that.

"Steven, there's no need to get upset-"

Steven disagreed. "For three years, we have been doing everything we can to make sure his condition doesn't worsen, and in one visit from Nathan Hayes, you've changed your mind?"

"No," I clarified. "He just offered a different perspective that had never occurred to me."

Steven crossed his arms over his chest. "Or, maybe, the more time Grant hangs out with Nathan Hayes, the more time you get to hang out with him, too."

My blood pressure spiked, and my blood started to boil.

"Did you seriously just accuse me of putting Grant's health at risk just to get Nathan Hayes' attention?" I couldn't believe how much I was seething inside. "Are you kidding me?"

"Are you telling me I'm wrong?"

"What I'm telling you is to get the hell out of my house," I snapped. "If that's what you think of me, get the hell out of my house and don't ever cross the threshold again." *I was pissed.* "You can drop Grant off at the door."

Steven's eyes narrowed. "The first time you suggest we let Grant go to ballgames, and it's so that Nathan Hayes can take him. Not *us.* But *Nathan Hayes.*" Steven stepped to me. "If Grant is finally going to go to a game, why wouldn't we be the ones to take him? Why Nathan Hayes?" He didn't let me answer. "Unless…" He let the sentence trail off, and I wanted to slap him.

"Let's clear something up, here and now," I seethed through clenched teeth. "I never said Nathan was going to take him to a game. I said Nathan *wanted* to take him to a game. And I mentioned Nathan's point of view because I thought it was worth discussing." I shook my head. "Of course, we'd be the ones to take Grant to his first live sports game ever. Do you honestly think I'd give that experience to someone else?"

Steven let out a deep breath and raked his fingers through his hair. His green eyes shot my way. "Maybe I just don't like the idea of you getting chummy with Nathan Hayes," he retorted.

I rolled my eyes. "You don't even know the man," I pointed out.

He cocked his head. "Well, maybe, I don't like the idea of you getting chummy with *any* man," he clarified, and my heart sank.

I understood exactly what Steven meant and that wasn't fair. He was overstepping. I knew it and he knew it, but men were stupid that way.

"You don't get to say that, Steven," I told him. "Especially, since you moved on from that part of our marriage and divorce ages ago."

I'll never forget the evening he had dropped Grant off, only to tell me he had started dating again. It was about eight months after our divorce had been finalized, and while I knew he'd eventually move on, it had still hurt. Not in a jealous, heartbroken way, but more of a stamp of finalization that our marriage was, indeed, over.

However, I had been grateful that he had told me, and I hadn't had to hear about it on social media or through gossip. And to his credit, he hadn't looked happy about the conversation, either. There was also the fact that it had taken him eight months, after our divorce, before he could bring himself to get back out there again.

It was hard when a divorce was due to irreconcilable differences. It was sad to know that we just hadn't been able to work things out. Our emotions had gotten the better of us, and we hadn't been able to climb out of the tangled web that had trapped us.

"Maybe not," he conceded. "But that doesn't change the way I feel, Andie."

"You don't get to be jealous, Steven," I repeated.

"I'm not jealous," he denied, then he let out a soft sigh. "I know I'm the reason we got divorced. *I know it.* But that doesn't mean I no longer care about you or feel the need to look out for you. You're still my family, Andie. You and Grant are still the most important things in the world to me. You will always be my son's mother, and I don't want to have to stand back and watch you get swept away by the likes of Nathan Hayes."

"The likes?" I choked out in a strangled laugh.

"C'mon, Andie," he grimaced. "A professional athlete? As beautiful as you are, I doubt the man's used to being monogamous." That was one thing I was never lacking with Steven. My confidence had been strong in our marriage because I knew Steven really believed me to be beautiful.

"And because of that very thing, I am positive Nathan Hayes is not interested in me, Steven," I reiterated. "The man can have anyone on the planet he wants. There's no way he wants a divorced mother of a young son."

Steven scoffed.

I grinned.

"Steven, he was just really impressed with how knowledgeable Grant was in sports," I told him. "He took an interest, and that is it."

Steven nodded, then dragged me into his arms in a tight hug. "Just be careful, Andie," he muttered in my hair.

"This is about Grant," I reassured him. "Just Grant."

Steven pulled back and gave me an unconvincing nod. "Look, I'll think about it this week," he promised. "But if we do this, then it's *us* taking him to his first game and it's going to be a football game." I smiled. "Since football is his favorite sport, that's what we'll give him. The regular season doesn't start until September, but that'll give us plenty of time to get tickets, or whatever."

I looked at him and knew that if this had been the Steven I had been dealing with when Grant had been diagnosed, we'd still be married. But no matter how far he's come, there was no way I could ever forget how cruel and self-absorbed he'd been that year following Grant's diagnosis.

We went back inside the house and Grant was watching Sports Center. When he saw us, he looked irritated. "They're talking about trading Grier Malone next season," he announced. "Who in their right mind would trade

Grier Malone?"

My brows rose. "And…"

"He's the best striker in soccer, Mom," he replied as if I should know this.

"Sometimes it's not about the talent, bud," Steven said. "Maybe he's not getting along with his teammates or something."

"It's not that hard to get along with people," he grumbled, but then he was just a kid. He didn't know yet that people sucked.

Steven looked over at me. "Do you mind if I hang out a bit?" It wasn't an odd request. Steven's hung out a few times since we moved here.

I nodded. "Sure." Then I went to the bedroom to get my Kindle, so that he and Grant could hang out in front of the television.

All things considered, it could be worse.

CHAPTER 10

Nathan ~

I had expected some friction, but not a full-blown argument.

But this little dude was really arguing with me.

"All I'm saying is that all those sports records aren't a true reflection of the player or players," Grant repeated, sounding all as if his opinion was fact.

"So, you're saying when a...quarterback throws for a pass that exceeds the previous record, it's bullsh-crap?"

"Apples and oranges," he replied, this time, sounding like he was eighteen instead of eight.

"Apples and oranges?"

The goddamn kid rolled his eyes at me. Currently, we were sitting in his living room while Andrea was making us lunch. It was Monday, and after allowing enough time to deem appropriate, I had been knocking on their door, ready to start my mentoring. Grant was lost and I needed to fix this.

"Only season records are accurate, Nathan," he said. He had started off our visit with some Mr. Hayes nonsense that I quickly squashed. Friends didn't need to be so formal with each other.

"How so?" I asked because the kid's logic was like a bad car wreck. I couldn't help but be fascinated.

"If I play football for only ten seasons, but you play for thirteen, well, of course, you're going to exceed my pass record, or touchdown record, or whatever. You played longer than I did," he replied without the 'duh', even though that was clearly implied in his tone. "The real measure is when you compare what you did within those ten years to what I did in those ten years."

Fuck, the kid had a point.

"But if we're talking stats or records within just the season and not a player's career length, well, those are more accurate because the time frame is the same. Apples, apples," he went on. "Specific timelines are the only real comparison. If I compare your rookie season with Hal Roberts' rookie season, then that's a fair comparison. But Hal has more seasons under his belt than you do."

"Okay, so then what happens to your theory if I've played fewer seasons than Hal, but break all his records?"

The little shit rolled his eyes at me again. "Nothing happens to my theory," he returned. "It's still the same concept. We'd be comparing your ten years to Hal's first ten years, and if you broke all his records, then you'd be better than him, clearly." Before I could comment, he continued with his lopsided logic. "And if a player plays five years longer than you did, but didn't break any of your records, then he sucks."

I stared at this kid who had more knowledge of sports than anyone I've ever met and was just blow the hell away. He was only eight, for fuck's sake.

"Why do you love sports so much?"

Grant scrunched of his face, and he looked to be giving it some real thought. Finally, he said, "I like that they're the best. Even if you're third-string, or whatever, you were still good enough to get there."

"Your mom doesn't like sports much, does she?" After the night she explained all about Grant's health issues, it had been hard to get up and walk out as if we were just casual friends. Hell, we weren't even really friends, at this point. We were friendly neighbors because I liked her son. But I couldn't deny my dick got hard at the thought of the woman, and she seemed just so refreshingly different from the women who've chased my pro-ball status.

Grant shrugged a shoulder. "She's a book editor," he said. "I think she likes books more." That would explain why she could work from home.

"What's your dad do?"

"He sells houses and buildings and things," he said, explaining what must be a real estate agent.

I nodded, letting him know I understood. "Your mom seems nice," I hedged. "But I still haven't met your dad."

"Dad stayed after on Sunday when he dropped me off," he casually mentioned, not realizing he'd just kicked my chest in. "If he stays next time, I can go get you."

"Does your dad stay the night a lot?" I was officially pumping an eight-year-old for information about his parents, and I'd have to say that this was a super new low in my life. But he mentioned it first, right?

Grant shook his head. "He doesn't stay the night," he clarified. "He just stays and hangs out with me a little more sometimes." Grant smiled big. "He says he misses me when I'm not with him."

"What's not to miss, bud?" I mean, seriously? This kid was awesome.

"Well, Mom misses me, too, when I'm not here, so they're just going to have to get used to sharing me," he stated, and I marveled at how much older this kid sounded when he spoke sometimes.

"Have they been sharing you long?" I inwardly cringed because this really was a new low, but I was interested in Andrea, so any little bit of information helped.

"Since I was six, I think," he replied, his face scrunched up again as if he were giving it some real thought.

Since he was six. Then that meant they've been separated and/or divorced for about two years. Of course, I couldn't get the details of their divorced from Grant, but I did need to know if there were some residual feelings there somewhere. I found myself attracted to Andrea, but I wasn't interested in a full-blown love triangle.

Grant paused Sports Center and turned to give me his undivided attention. "Guess what?"

"What?" I was just as eager to hear what he had to say as he was to say it.

"When Mom and Dad were out on the balcony yesterday, I went to go get a juice pack and I could hear them through the door."

"And what did you hear?"

"Mom asked Dad if I could go to a real ballgame," he almost squealed like a teenage girl. "Dad said he would think about it. Isn't that awesome?"

My chest was a starburst of warmth. "That is awesome," I told him. And it was. I couldn't wait to take him to a game.

"Dad told her that if I get to go, him and Mom will take me to my first game," he went on. "And it's going to be a football game in September!" he finished excitedly.

"That's gre-"

Wait.

What?

They're going to take him? And it's going to be football?

"I wouldn't mind going to an Angels' game, but I agree with my Dad," he prattled on as if he hadn't just broken my goddamn heart. "Since football is my favorite, I want my first game to be football."

I shook my head and tried to prioritize. "Yeah, about that," I grimaced. "Why is football your favorite?"

"Because offensive linemen can get away without running if they don't have to," he said, and I could actually hear my heart cracking down the middle. "If I could play anything, it would be that position because there's not a lot of running." The goddamn kid scrunched his face up again. "Or a hockey goalie. I think I could do that, too."

My phone rang, saving me from crying all over the place like a fucking pussy, and when I picked it up off the coffee table, I thanked God for the call.

I looked at Grant. "I have to take this."

He grinned and unpaused Sports Center. "No problem."

"What's up?" I said into the phone.

"I'm dancing through your town next week. Wednesday and Thursday, so I can stop by and see your Mom," Sergio said. "I'm going to stop by and see you, too." He didn't ask, but then he was my best friend and didn't need to. Next to my brothers, Sergio Hernandez was my closest friend.

"Sounds good," I replied.

"Sounds good," he echoed. "Gotta go. I got a blonde winking at me." He hung up as I laughed into the phone. I knew the blonde was his wife.

Andrea walked in with a platter of sandwiches as I pocketed my phone. "Anybody hungry?"

"I am," Grant immediately replied.

"Same here," I told her, and she smiled as she set the platter on the coffee table. She even put down a water for me and a juice pack for Grant.

"You guys having fun?"

Before Grant could answer, I said, "Can Grant come by next Wednesday? Sergio Hernandez is going to be in town."

Grant's little head whipped around, his eyes wide, while Andrea asked, "Who's Sergio Hernandez?"

Grant turned to her. "Mom, I think we really need to talk," he said, shaking his head sadly.

"He's right," I added. "This is starting to become embarrassing."

CHAPTER 11

Andrea ~

I didn't see this coming.

Once again, Nathan Hayes was in my living room, taking liberties with Grant's life, and I was surprised this shit was still shocking me. Especially, since it was a Friday night. Didn't Nathan Hayes have anything better to do than butt into an eight-year-old's life?

"Are you trying to bargain with me?" I asked, listening to the words he was saying, but still in disbelief.

"What's wrong with that?" he challenged.

"Uh, other than the fact that Grant is not your son and you don't really have a say in anything we decided for him, I suppose nothing," I replied sardonically.

"Tell me how that's not a fair trade?" he pushed again.

We were standing in the middle of my living room again, squaring off, and it was really blowing my mind. "Because you don't have rights where Grant is concerned," I tried again. "You do understand that he's not yours, right?" Maybe Nathan *was* a lunatic and the MLB forced him to retire early because he couldn't hide it from them anymore.

"He's my friend," Nathan insisted like a petulant child. "If you're going to rob me of the experience of taking him to his first ballgame ever, then the least you could do is let me take him to his first baseball game ever." He looked like he was on the verge of a legit tantrum. "You guys can have football," he grumbled.

"How do you even know we've talked about taking him to a game?" I asked, wondering if the man has planted bugs in my house.

He immediately looked guilty, and bugs were suddenly a real possibility. He grimaced a bit as he said, "He kind of overheard you and your ex-husband talking about it Sunday when you guys were out on the balcony," he informed me. "He knows you guys are thinking of taking him."

My heart sank at the news.

I threw my finger up to stop Nathan from speaking and pulled out my phone. Steven answered on the third ring. "Hey," he said. "You okay?" I rarely called when he had Grant because I didn't like intruding on their time together.

"Yeah," I assured him quickly. "I just wanted to warn you that Grant overheard some of our conversation, Sunday. He knows we're thinking of taking him to a game."

"How do you know?" he asked, concern lacing his question.

"Nathan told me," I admitted. "I guess Grant told him." There was some heavy silence on Steven's end, and I didn't like the anxious feeling it gave me. "Steven?"

"I'm getting really tired of hearing Nathan Hayes' name when it comes to making decisions about Grant, Andie," he said, and I really couldn't blame him. Hadn't I just been thinking and saying the same thing?

"It's not like that, Steven," I semi-fibbed. "Grant told him what he overheard, and that's it." I could feel Nathan tense next to me, but I paid him no mind. I had bigger issues to deal with.

Steven let out a sigh. "Give me a sec," he said, then I heard him telling Grant he was stepping outside for a second. After hearing a door shut, Steven said, "I plan on telling him this weekend that we're taking him to a game." I couldn't help my smile. "I looked up the season openers and the Raiders are playing the Chargers for their first game of the season."

"He's going to love that," I said, knowing Grant was going to be over the moon when Steven told him.

"We'll talk about it more when I drop him off on Sunday, okay?"

"Okay," I replied, realizing now was not the time to discuss this with Nathan standing only a few feet away from me. "I'll talk to you later."

"Talk to you later, Andie," he returned before hanging up.

"Problems?" Nathan asked and I side-eyed him. "What?" Yeah, that innocent act was not working.

"Look, Nathan, I really appreciate you taking an interest in Grant, but you're crossing lines," I told him. "I have no problem with you befriending Grant, but you have no rights to him." My brows drew downward. "And you do realize how bizarre this all is, right?"

"Because I want to take him to a game?"

I shook my head. "Because you're *insisting* on taking him to a game," I corrected.

Nathan went back to being serious. "Look, Andrea-"

"Andie is fine, Nathan," I graciously allowed. We might not be friends, but we were becoming something.

Nathan smiled, and he really was too good-looking for any woman's peace of mind. "I just really like Grant," he said. "I'm not trying to be a dick, I swear. I just find the kid so goddamn interesting, and I really like hanging out with him."

I thought about that, and while I still believed he was being overboard, I also believed Steven was being overly sensitive about Nathan Hayes befriending Grant. Grant loved sports. They were his number one passion, and while Grant loved Steven, Steven was probably feeling threatened by Grant hanging out with someone who Grant hailed as a hero. It was hard for a parent to compete with their child's hero.

"I'll talk to Steven, but you have to promise to stay on the side of respectability, Nathan," I warned him. "If we don't want Grant doing something, I expect you to honor that."

I watched as he chewed on his bottom lip. He looked to really be thinking about it, and it made me wonder if we really did live next to a madman. Who didn't think they needed to respect a child's parents' wishes? It shouldn't have been that hard to agree to.

"How respectable?" Nathan asked, throwing me off.

"What?"

And then this soap opera took another turn into the strange when Nathan stepped to me and dipped his head to create an intimacy that had my heart thumping and body parts clenching.

Oh.

My.

Goodness.

"I mean, how respectable do I have to behave around you?" he asked, and there no mistaking his meaning. I might be in the middle of a dry spell, but I wasn't that clueless.

"Nathan-" He stepped closer, stopping my words mid-sentence, and his body heat almost made me moan. Back to that dry spell, I missed sex. I hadn't been lying to Rachel when I had told her that.

"See, the thing is," he began, his voice a dark rumble, "as fascinating as Grant is, he's not the only person in this house that I come over to see."

Oh, God.

Nathan Hayes was hitting on me, and I was not equipped to handle something like this. I'd never been a casual sex kind of person, and while I wasn't opposed to it, I've never had to navigate through the concept before. The men I've slept with had always been boyfriends or was Steven. Could I have a fling with Nathan Hayes?

Probably.

Except for two very important factors...

"Nathan, I'm not sure this is a good idea," I squeaked. "If this...turns sour, you're my neighbor. Plus, there's your friendship with Grant to consider." Was I looking the man in the eyes as I delivered my little speech? Nope. Was it cowardly? Yep. But was it necessary? Absolutely. There was no way I'd be able to resist those baby blues filled with heat and wicked promises. So, rather than look directly into the sun, blinding myself stupid, I stared at his chest. Which, admittedly, wasn't much better since the man was built like a god.

"And you're positive it's going to turn sour?" he asked the top of my head.

Yes.

"Uh, pretty sure," I replied. "Besides, don't you have…dates you can take out or something?"

He chuckled and I felt it all the way to my bones. "No, Andie," he rasped out. "I don't have *dates* I can take out or something. There's only one woman I'm interested in taking out."

I took a step back to give myself some thinking room, but that failed spectacularly when Nathan stepped with me.

Quit being a coward.

I looked up at the gorgeous man and hit him with the truth. "Nathan, I don't have the time, patience, or level of self-esteem it takes to date someone like you," I said, hoping I didn't sound like a complete loser. "I've never had a one-night stand, and I'm pretty sure I wouldn't be able to handle you just in general." I cleared my throat. "So, while I appreciate the interest, uh, I'm going to have to say no."

"No?"

"No," I confirmed with a confident nod. "Thank you, but no."

CHAPTER 12

Nathan ~

I didn't see this coming.

Sure, I knew she'd have concerns over my friendship with Grant, and that she might even suspect I was befriending her son just so I could get into her pants, but I hadn't anticipated a flat-out no. Ego aside, no wasn't a word I heard often.

I stepped back and gave her some room. I wasn't a total dick. I knew I was running roughshod over her and her son, but the kid was fucking awesome, so who wouldn't want to hang out with him? And Andie was fucking gorgeous, so who wouldn't want to take her out on a date?

"I'm not the type of man who would put a child in the middle of something like a breakup, Andie," I told her.

The woman scoffed. "And how in the hell would I know that?" she returned. "I don't *know* you, Nathan."

"Well, what better way than to get to know me than a date?" I fired back.

"We become friends," she tossed out like that was totally acceptable.

"I don't want to just be your friend," I said, going for honestly. Might as well put it all out there.

Andie let out a deep breath. "Nathan, I'm not opposed to casual sex, but it's not anything I've ever-"

I swung my palms up to stop her. "Whoa, hold up," I interrupted. "Who says I want to have casual sex with you? I asked you on a goddamn date, Andie. Not to meet me in some seedy motel."

She winced. "All the same-"

"No." I shook my head. "It's not all the same. If I wanted casual sex, I'd hit up a bar or something."

Andie regarded me for a second before her brow drew downward. "Nope," she said. "I'm not buying it."

"Buying what?"

"As you and Grant are so fond of telling me, you're Nathan Hayes. I find it hard to believe that a divorced mother of an eight-year-old is what does it for you."

Okay.

Now I was getting irritated.

"Because that's all you are?" I challenged.

Her head reared back in confusion. "What?"

"Is that all you are?" I repeated. "Are you only a divorced mother of an eight-year-old?" Andie still looked confused. "Or are you Andrea? Do you have your own interested? A job? Friends? Or does your life revolve around Grant and your ex-husband only?" She bristled and I knew I hit a sore spot. "Because the woman I think you are does do it for me. And the fact that she's a mother of a young boy and has an ex-husband is irrelevant. They're not bad things, and they aren't enough to make me not want to get to know the woman you are who is independent of being a mother and someone's ex-wife."

She let out a deep sigh. "Nathan, you have to look at this from my point of view," she argued. "You're a professional baseball player. The life you live-"

I let out a dark laugh. "The life I live?" I chuckled, though there was no humor in it. "I live a life where I retired early, so I could enjoy my golden years and not spend them suffering through years of aches and pains. I live a life where my brother, Gideon, calls me and cusses me out if I don't call our mother at least once a week. I live a life where I returned to my hometown to live. Not L.A., or New York City, or Atlanta, or anywhere that's for twenty-somethings. I live a life where my other brother, Sayer, calls to warn me that his stepdaughter is going to interview me for some high school history exposé article." Her face softened, and I appreciated that she was hearing me out. "If I wanted strippers, or models, or champagne bottles at three in the morning, I sure as hell wouldn't have moved back here, Andie."

"Nath-"

"Oh, and my father's still tough enough and strong enough to kick all three of our asses if we upset my mother," I added.

"Nath-"

"My brother married the love of his life in April, but she comes with a douchebag ex-husband we all have to play nice with as to not upset his stepdaughter, Leta," I continued. "Gideon's a complete dick on a good day. And the only real friend, *true friend,* I still have from my playing days is Sergio Hernandez, because he's a family man and he gets not wanting to live in the fast lane until you wreck."

"Nath-"

"So, don't stand there and tell me it's odd, or strange, or unrealistic for me to be interested in you, because none of that's true," I kept prattling on. "I think you're beautiful. I like seeing how you love your son. I respect how you get along with his father. And even though I know nothing about your divorce, it's clear you and your ex-husband have put that difficult experience behind you guys to do what's best for your son." I let out an irritated scoff. "I don't mind baggage, Andie, because that means you're real people. You've had real experiences, and they're deeper than making sure you get the best suite at The Four Seasons."

"Nathan!"

"What?!"

Andie closed her eyes and let out another deep breath. I noticed she did that a lot when she talked to me. Opening her eyes again, she said. "You do realize that Steven's going to think you're using Grant to sleep with me?"

I nodded because I knew there was that possibility. Hell, I thought she would think it when I had made my intentions clear. "But do *you* think that?"

She shook her head. "No," she answered. "It's obvious you don't need to resort to games or hurtful tactics for sex, but Steven's going to have a hard time with this."

"So?" I asked. "You're divorced, right?"

"Well, yeah," she muttered.

"Then he'll have to get over it, right?" Then a thought occurred to me. "Unless there's still something going on betw-"

Andie shook her head. "No," she denied. "It's nothing like that. Steven moved on ages ago. I think…Nathan, you'd be the first guy I've dated since my divorce. And while Steven doesn't have a say, we still care about each other."

"Care about each other?" *What in the fuck did that mean?*

"Our divorce was rough," she said, "but we managed to get past the pain. And I'm not going to stand here and lie to you and tell you he's a distant mistake or something cold like that." She had a fond look in her eyes. "He was once a man I loved enough to spend the rest of my life with. And while life had other plans, I'm not going to demote him to a mistake or a regret. I care about him and I want him happy. He's the father of my child, and the best thing I can do for my child is to make sure his father is happy in life."

My chest felt like it'd just been kicked in. "You're still in love with him, aren't you?"

She smiled as she shook her head. "No," she chuckled. "I am not in love with him anymore, but I value what we have. There are too many separated families out there that don't get along and are damaging their children because of it. I am grateful that Grant's parents care enough about him and each other not to force him to live in a toxic environment."

I immediately thought of my sister-in-law and her ex-husband and her words painted a clearer picture of what she was trying to convey. She didn't need or particularly care if she had her ex-husband's permission to date me, but it'd be nice if she had it. For everyone's sake.

"Talk to him, then let me know what day works for you," I relented.

She arched a brow. "That confident, are you?"

Fuck it.

I stepped to her, slid my hands into her sun-kissed locks, and brought my lips down on hers. Andie let out a surprised squeal, but all that did was give me access into her sweet, hot mouth. My tongue found its way in, and when I felt her hands grab at the fabric of my shirt, I deepened the kiss and there was no way I was letting her ex-husband stop whatever this could become.

Andie Miller tasted fucking divine.

I couldn't say how long the kiss lasted, but when I finally pulled back, she looked dazed, and her lips were swollen with use.

I bet she looked fucking magnificent when she came undone.

"So," I said, releasing her hair, "talk with Steven, and then let me know what day works best for you."

While Andie might look wrecked, her mind was still sharp as ever. "I think you're going to be more trouble than you're worth, Nathan Hayes," she mumbled.

I grinned down at her. "I think you might be right."

CHAPTER 13

Andrea ~

I was a grown ass woman. I shouldn't be this nervous.

But I was.

When Steven had dropped Grant off on Sunday, everything had been perfect. Grant had run inside to tell me all about how Steven had gotten us tickets to the season opener of the Raiders versus the Chargers. He told me all about how, together, he and Steven had picked which hotel we'd be staying at and how they had made sure to get adjoining suites, so Grant could go back and forth between rooms during the weekend. I'd never seen him so excited, and I had felt guilty for keeping the experience from him for so long.

After he had rambled on about anything and everything to do with the game, he had gone to his room to get ready for his bath, and that had left me and Steven to talk. I had offered to pay for half of everything, but Steven had insisted that it was his treat. I was thinking he probably felt guiltier about our decision to not let Grant go to live games than I did.

When all the details had been hashed out, I had wanted to talk to Steven about Nathan asking me out, but I had chickened out, not wanting to ruin the good vibe we had going on Sunday. And it wasn't that I needed Steven's permission to date, but I didn't want to fight with him over it, either.

I stared at my phone in my hand. Right now, Grant and Nathan were sitting out on the balcony, visiting with Nathan's former teammate and friend, Sergio Hernandez. I could hear muffled laughs and surprised cries through the sliding glass door, but that was about it. After making Nathan swear on all that was holy that he wouldn't swear or tell grownup tales, I pretended not to hover and let them have some guy time.

Grant had been ecstatic.

I let out a deep breath and sent the text.

Me: *R u busy?*

Steven: *Just going thru some listings. Everything ok?*

Me: *Do u have a second 2 talk?*

The phone rang in my hand and I quickly answered it. My nerves were clearly messing with me, but that kiss had been knee-weakening, and I wanted to do it again. "Hello?"

"Hey," Steven replied. "Everything okay?"

"Yeah," I grumbled because I really did feel stupid. "I…" I took a deep breath. "Nathan asked me out on a date last week. And…and I want to say yes."

He was quiet for so long, I wondered if he was going to say anything at all. Finally, he asked, "You don't think that might make things complicated for Grant if it…doesn't work out?"

I didn't want to bring up old hurts, but as I spoke with Steven something became painfully clear. "Steven, Grant aside, nothing in the world can ever hurt me worse than our divorce," I told him truthfully.

"Andie-"

"No, just listen," I said, interrupting. "Our divorce was extremely painful for the both of us, Steven. I'm not placing blame, or taking blame, or anything like that. But if we can still be cordial and civil and care for one another, for the sake of our son, I can be cordial and civil with my neighbor for Grant's sake, if he ends up using me and dumping me."

"Andie," he growled, "don't talk about yourself like that."

"The point *is,*" I stressed, "even if it doesn't work out, it won't be as painful as getting over what I've already had to with our divorce."

"He's a professional baseball player, Andie," Steven groaned.

"I know." And I did. I understood Steven's concerns because I'd had them myself. "But it's just a date. It could lead to something or absolutely nothing, but I want to find out."

He was quiet for a few seconds before saying, "Okay." I smiled. "Just be careful, Andie," he added. "I know this sounds stupid coming from the one man who has hurt you the most, but I don't want to see you get hurt." My heart lurched. I wished all divorced parents could care for each other the way Steven and I still did.

"I know, Steven," I replied. "Neither do I. But what does it get me to play it safe?"

I could hear him sighing over the phone. "Okay. Just keep it separate from Grant's friendship with Nathan until you're absolutely sure about where it's going."

"Of course," I immediately agreed. That was a given with or without Steven mentioning it.

"Thank you for talking to me about this first, Andie," he said softly.

"It's no more than you deserve for giving me the same courtesy last year," I replied.

"I'll talk to you later, okay?"

"Okay." I hung up, and a sudden rush of emotion hit me.

Even though it was over between me and Steven, dating someone new was just another step towards walking away from the life I once believed I'd always have. The arguing had been the first step. Steven sleeping in the spare bedroom had been the second step. Steven moving out of our house had been the third step. Me filing for legal separation had been the fourth step. Me filing for divorce had been the fifth step. Moving into new homes, leaving our old one behind, had been the sixth step. Steven going out on his first date had been the seventh step. And now I was taking the final step by going out on my first date.

Well, I suppose that wasn't exactly true.

The final step will be if Steven or I ever get married again. Now, granted, I wasn't looking to get married ever again, but I wasn't going to put restrictions on my heart, my love, or my life's possibilities.

Getting my sentimentality under control, I headed towards the kitchen and peeked out the sliding glass door. Grant, Nathan, and Sergio were laughing at something, a joke probably, and they all looked happy.

Grant looked happy.

I walked through the kitchen and slid the door open. All three male heads turned my way. I smiled. "Having fun?"

"I'm being ganged up on," Nathan retorted, and Sergio and Grant laughed.

"He's got a point, Nate," Sergio chuckled. "It's hard to argue logic and facts." Sergio put his hand out to fist bump Grant. Grant's smile was a mile wide as he fist bumped a professional baseball player.

"Yeah, well, the kid still likes football better than baseball, so he can't be all that smart," Nathan grumbled.

"Hockey and baseball are pretty neck and neck right now," Grant announced, and Nathan looked pained while Sergio barked out another laugh.

"You're killing me, kid," Nathan breathed out. "Absolutely killing me."

I smiled. "Lunch will be ready in a few," I told them before winking at my son. "Go easy on them, kiddo."

Grant smiled his father's smile. "I'll try."

I went back inside and got to making some lunch. Lunch was always easy with fruit platters or sandwiches. Then I chuckled as I realized I was putting together a simple lunch for freakin' professional baseball players.

Jesus.

A few minutes later, I was placing all the ingredients on the counter when I heard the sliding glass door slide open. I looked up and Nathan was walking towards me, a huge grin on his face. "Hey."

"Hey," I said, smiling back.

"Does Friday night work for you?" he asked, not pussy footing around.

"Careful, Nathan," I said softly. "You're sounding a bit cocky."

Nathan smirked, and it looked good on him. "Confident," he corrected.

I decided to put the man out of his misery. "Friday night is fine."

"Where would you like to go?"

While his question was perfectly normal, it gave me pause. If I was going to take baby steps and keep Grant protected from what could possibly become a disaster, I couldn't very well go out in public with Nathan. Even being back in his hometown, cozy and quiet, people would see us and might take pictures or whatever. I wasn't ready for that kind of publicity yet, if ever.

"How about I cook dinner?" I suggested. "Photographers-"

"*I'll* cook dinner at my place," he offered. "And I get it, Andie."

I gave him a small nod. "Dinner at your place, then."

"Dinner at my place," he repeated before heading back out onto the balcony.

CHAPTER 14

Nathan ~

I was a grown ass man. I shouldn't be this nervous.

But I was.

Maybe it was because this wasn't some woman following me up to my hotel room after a win and taking it for what it was. This wasn't a fan tossing every compliment out there in an attempt to lure me with flattery. Christ, Andie had no idea who I was when we first met, and she's hardly been impressed since finding out.

I've never dated before. I've slept with my fair share of women, but I've never dated anyone past my junior year in college when the MLB had become a real possibility. I hadn't wanted to divide my attention between proving my talents to my team and proving my faithfulness to a girlfriend back home. I wanted to be worth the money I was being paid and I wanted to deserve the adoration of the fans.

Now, had I been madly in love at the time I had made that decision, that decision might not have been made, but I hadn't been. And I'd seen too much cheating in my playing years to know that I would have lost my concentration of the game had I been seriously involved with someone. I would have spent all my spare time convincing my girl or wife that I was being faithful, and not because she would have been the insecure one, but because *I* would have been. The last thing I'd ever want my wife to fear was my faithfulness.

So, Andie was the first woman I've ever asked on a date, and she was the first woman who came without an underlining understanding that she was expected to leave before the sun came up the next morning. Not that sex was on the table for tonight, because I knew it wasn't.

I knocked on Andie's door and waited as patiently as I could until she answered the door. All day, I'd been promising myself that I'd act the perfect gentleman tonight, but that kiss has been haunting me since the second I had walked out of her condo after kissing her. Her reaction hadn't been fake or overexaggerated to spare my fragile professional baseball player's ego. She hadn't sworn it was the best kiss of her life, which, admittedly, the best kiss of her life should be the one she shared with Steven on their wedding day, but I didn't want to think about that. His loss, my gain, and all that jazz.

The door swung open, and I almost swallowed my tongue.

Jesus fucking Christ.

Andie's golden hair was loose around her shoulders and the goddamn strands looked like they were shimmering. Her makeup was minimal, but effective. Her brown eyes seemed darker, her cheeks looked pinker, and her lips seemed thicker.

Looking my fill, the woman was dressed in a simple light green blouse with a dark black skirt and black heels. However, the blouse wasn't gaping, the skirt wasn't tight, and the heels weren't hooker-inch. The outfit was perfectly respectable and there was nothing provocative about it.

Well, except for the woman wearing it.

Andie looked beautiful, alluring, and seductive, and the woman wasn't even trying. We were having dinner at my house, and while she had put in the effort to look nice, she hadn't gone overboard. Andie got ready for a dinner date with Nate, not a dinner date with Nathan Hayes.

Pretty sure I was standing in Andie's doorway falling a little bit in love with the woman.

"You look beautiful," I told her truthfully. "Absolutely beautiful."

She cocked her head to the side a bit and gave me a small smile. "Thank you, Nathan," she replied. "You look very nice, also."

Then something occurred to me. "You know, you can call me Nate if you want to." I couldn't believe I hadn't given her that leeway after she had said it was okay for me to call her Andie. Especially, since her son has been calling me Nate for the past few days now.

"Nate," she muttered softly, as if trying to see how the name tasted on her lips. Then she smiled wide. "Which do you prefer?"

"I'll answer to both, but Nathan Hayes is for the public. Nate is what my family and friends call me," I told her.

"Can I go with what just feels right in the moment?" she asked, and I liked that question.

"Absolutely."

Andie smiled. "Let me grab my purse," she said quickly, and I stepped just inside the doorway as she walked back towards the bedrooms to get her purse.

When she emerged from the hallway, I asked, "Ready?"

She nodded. "Yep."

I escorted her towards the elevators, and even though it was only one flight up, all kinds or sordid thoughts popped into my mind about just her and me in the elevator.

Aaaaaaaaaaaaannnnnnnnnd my dick was starting to get hard.

I did my best to tamp down my raging hormones and followed Andie into the elevator. Inserting my key into the penthouse lock, I pressed the button. Riding up the one floor in complete silence, I wondered, for the first time, if my wealth was going to be a mark against me with a woman. Andie wasn't the type of woman who was impressed with flash, and I hoped she didn't view my penthouse as flashy, rather than just my home.

The elevator doors opened, and I placed my hand on the small of her back, guiding her into an open foyer. There were a pair of cushioned benches arched on either side of the foyer with a huge fake plotted plant in the middle.

Andie glanced around. "Are those for…guests?"

I shook my head as I led her towards the front door. "No. They're for decorative purposes," I answered her. "Although, I've never had any guests here, so I dunno."

Andie stopped. "What do you mean?"

"I've only been living here about three months," I told her, pushing open the front door and guiding her in. "The only people who have been here are my parents, my bothers, and Sergio, whenever he's in town."

"Is it weird that you've been here three months and I've never seen you?"

"Not really," I said, shutting the door behind us. "The penthouse comes with its own elevator that goes directly to the condominium garage, so that's the one I use as I come and go. Also, until recently, I spent a lot of time at my parents making up for all my traveling." Andie grinned at me and it surprised me. She wasn't checking out my place like most people would have been. She was looking at me as if learning something about me was more important than guesstimating how much the penthouse was worth.

"Your mom missed you a lot, I take it?"

"You have no idea," I chuckled.

"I have a son," she laughed. "I have a pretty good idea."

After hanging up her purse on one of the coat hooks near the door, I smiled at her and grabbed her hand. We made our way through the sitting room, and then the living room. "I hope you like Italian," I said, then looked down at her. "I guess I should have asked beforehand."

Andie grinned up at me. "I love Italian," she replied, opting not to make me suffer.

We reached the kitchen and I pulled out a chair for her. "Have a seat while I get the food." I had already placed out the plates and silverware and wine glasses, all we needed was the food.

"So, you've only been here three months?"

"Yeah," I answered as I delivered the food to the table. "Even though I had made the decision to retire at the end of last season, I hadn't been quite ready to walk away completely."

"I bet," she said. "Walking away from the life you had into a completely new one can be intimidating."

"It was," I agreed. "Kind of still is, if I'm being honest."

"So, why this place?"

"It's more than I need, for sure," I admitted. "But I wanted privacy while I figured out my next move. Buying a house where neighbors went out and did their yards and waved to each other at their mailboxes was too wild a concept for me at the time. I'm still winding down, I suppose."

"I can understand that," she replied. "Sometimes quiet is the only thing you need."

I turned to face her, two bottles of wine in my hands. "Red or white?"

"Red, or course," she scoffed.

"Of course," I laughed. I poured her a glass and did the same for myself. I served her before taking a seat and serving myself.

"Everything looks perfect, Nate," she said, and my chest kicked as she called me Nate.

"Good," I said. "I'm glad."

Then she eyed me. "Did you cook this or did your Mom stop by?"

I barked out a laugh. "I cooked it," I assured her. "My mom was a stay-at-home mother, but she felt men needed to know how to wash a dish just as much as they needed to know how to mow a lawn."

"Your mom sounds awesome."

I shook my head. "The woman's batshit crazy."

CHAPTER 15

Andrea ~

Screw taking it slow.

Dinner had been perfect. The conversation had been perfect. The entire date had been perfect.

Nathan had told me all about his brothers and parents and how he got to become a professional baseball player. He retold stories that had me laughing until my sides were hurting. A lot of them had included his brothers when they were younger, but there were some from his playing days. He had told me all about how Sergio had become his best friend and how he absolutely adored Sergio's family.

I had ended up telling him all about my parents and brother, and how Justin now owned and operated the family bar, while my parents were living up the retired life. I had told him all about being a book editor and how I've written a couple of books myself. I had also told him all about Rachel and her family and how they were like my second family.

We had ended the evening's conversations with Grant and his condition. To my surprise, Nathan had read up on interstitial lung disease and he had asked questions as if he were truly interested in what needed to be done for Grant. It had been sweet and my complete undoing.

Why my undoing, you ask?

Because the night was wrapping up and I wanted nothing more than to jump this gorgeous, generous, entertaining lunatic.

Knowing Nathan wouldn't say no if I offered up my body had me really, really re-thinking one-night stands and reevaluating just how bad an idea it might be to jump my neighbor. While everything I had told Steven was true in regard to if a relationship with Nathan went south, I still knew this was dangerous territory I was embarking on. I wanted my decision to be a confident one. I didn't want it made because I was horny as hell, plain and simple. It's been over two years, and my body was *craving* what it knew

Nathan Hayes could do for it.

Then I inwardly cringed at the thought of throwing myself at him on the first date. Nathan was probably used to women throwing themselves at him with no shame, and here I was, contemplating doing the same.

I'd be just like all those other women who chased famous dick.

I jumped out of my seat. "Uh, this was great," I muttered. "Do...do you need help with the dishes or cleaning up? I can-" I stopped talking and reached for my plate and wine glass.

Nathan stood up and walked over, placing his hand on my wrist. "Put it down," he said warily. "I can clean up."

I refused to look at him. "But I can help," I insisted. "It's not fair for you to cook *and* clean." I went to pull my arm away, but his hand tightened around my wrist.

"Andie, is everything okay?"

"Yeah, yep, yes," I stuttered like a fool. "It's just getting late and all. We should clean up and I should probably go."

Nathan let go of my wrist but took the plate and wine glass from my hands. After he set them back down on the table, he said, "It's not even eight yet."

I still refused to look at him, and just kept prattling on. "Early to bed, early to rise, and all that," I remarked like a loser. "Sleep is the recharging of the soul, you know."

"I, uh, didn't know," he mumbled all confused.

"Yeah, so...." I didn't finish with my nonsense. I started walking towards the front door to grab my purse when a strong hand reached out and wrapped around my arm, stopping me. Resolving myself to stop being a coward, I looked up at him. "I..."

He regarded me through narrowed eyes. "What's going on, Andie?"

This. Was. Embarrassing.

"I...I just think I bett...better go," I replied lamely. "It's getting late."

Nathan let go of my arm and his face fell into disappointment. "You didn't have a good time," he surmised *incorrectly*.

I couldn't let him think that. "I had a lovely time, Nate," I told him honestly. "Everything was perfect. Really."

He didn't believe me. "Then why are you rushing out of here like you can't get away from me fast enough?"

I wanted to lie.

Christ, how I wanted to lie.

But I couldn't.

"This is so embarrassing," I mumbled.

"What is?"

I stared up at Nathan and I knew I was going to have to humiliate myself in front of this gorgeous man. He's been nothing but great all night long and I truly did have a great time. I couldn't let him believe I hadn't.

"IfIdontgetoutofhererightnowImgoingtojumpyourboneslikeadesperatetramp," I rushed out like a complete neurotic mess.

Nathan stilled. "Uh, excuse me?"

And because my humiliation knew no bounds and was trying to go for the gold, the shamelessness just came pouring out. "I was sitting there, looking at you and realizing what a good time I've had, and then those thoughts started giving way to *bad* thoughts, and then those thoughts started giving way to how you're probably so used to women throwing themselves at you, I'd just be another tramp on the VIP list of women who've just rolled over for you, and I realized I had to get the hell out of here before I became one of those women," I rushed out, stopping only long enough to take a breath. "And I don't want to be one of those women, Nate. I like you. I really, really like you, even if you are a bit of a lunatic, so I need to get out of here, because if I don't, I'm going to go all trampy on you. And it's been over two years, Nate. Count them. *Two. Years.* I'm not sure I won't just go rabid on you, and then what?" He looked like he was going to say something, but I just. Couldn't. Shut. The. Hell. Up. "I'll tell you then what. You'll think I'm nothing but one of *them.* You'll think I slept with you for your fame or money, because who sleeps with a guy on the first date when she's been playing hard to get the entire time?" Again, he looked like he wanted to say something, but I didn't let him. "Women who haven't had sex in over two years, that's who. Me, Nate. And that makes me no better than-"

"Andrea!" he bit out forcefully, and I wanted the ground to swallow me up.

"Y...yeah?"

He was looking like he wanted to smile, and if he did, I was going to pack up our condo and move. "I was only hoping for a kiss at the end of the night," he said, and I knew he was laughing at me on the inside. "But I'm totally all for the jumping portion of the evening."

"Nath-"

He stepped forward and took my face in his hands. "I am *dying* for you to go all rabid tramp on me, Andie. Literally, dying for it, baby."

Oh, Sweet Jesus, he called me baby.

"Nathan-"

"And you're out of your mind if you think I'd ever confuse you for an athlete chaser, Andie," he continued. "I've paid attention these past couple of weeks and I know you're nothing like that."

"But even if I'm not using you for your fame or money, Nathan, trust me when I say, this first night, I would totally be using you for your body. Two years," I reminded him.

"Then use me," he said roughly before slamming his lips down on mine, and all good intentions not to be a hussy flew out the window. I was going to ride Nathan Hayes into the sunrise.

I wrapped my arms around his neck, but because he was so much taller than I was, he grabbed the back of my thighs and lifted me until my legs were anchored around his waist. This made our bodies align better and the kiss deepened as I felt the hardness that was Nathan Hayes rub up against the center of my panties.

And Holy Mary, Mother of God.

Do you know what you get when you're faced with six-foot-four of conditioned muscle? What I'm guessing to be at least eight to nine inches of hard penis. Nathan's dick felt like a baseball bat between my opened legs and the metaphor wasn't lost on me at all.

His large hands cupping my ass, Nathan broke off the kiss and latched his lips and teeth onto my neck. In between my moans and his nips against my skin, he said, "I'm going to fuck you, good and deep, all night long, Andrea."

He called me Andrea, and my heart broke into a rapid tattoo of emotions. This wasn't casual where I was Andie and he was Nate. This was going to mean something and that thought scared the shit out of me.

But not enough to stop.

CHAPTER 16

Nathan ~

Screw taking it slow.

My mind was telling me it was too soon to be in love with this woman, but my heart and dick were convinced they were.

And the fact that she thought sleeping with me on the first night made her a tramp was endearing. I didn't personally view women that way, but Andie was cute as fuck with her lopsided logic. I was a firm believer that if it was tacky to sleep with a man on the first date, then it was tacky to sleep with a woman on the first date. Men did not have the monopoly on sexual urges.

I also knew that while she might think it, she wasn't using me for my body. If she were all about satisfying her sexual urges, she wouldn't have gone two years without sex. Hell, she'd still be sleeping with her ex if it were all about scratching the itch. But she'd done neither, so this was more than sex.

But I'd already known that.

She moaned at my filth, so I kept going. "I'm not going to stop until there isn't a position left that I haven't fucked you in."

"Oh, God," she breathed, tilting her head to give me more access.

I walked her towards my bedroom, and I prayed with every step that she wouldn't change her mind. I wanted my dick buried in this woman more than I've ever wanted anything else in my life. She was pretty close to passing up playing in the MLB as the best things that have ever happened to me.

And, God, how I wanted to taste her.

We reached the bedroom and as soon as I laid her on the bed, I dropped to my knees, grabbed her by her hips, and yanked her to the edge of the bed.

"Nathan…" Determined not to give her time to change her mind, I spread her legs wide open, thanked everything under the sun for the invention of skirts, and started kissing the inside of her left thigh. Her hands slid into my hair. "Oh, God…"

I hooked her panties to the side because the two seconds it would have taken for me to slide her panties down were two seconds too many. I was greeted with a pair of wet, swollen, pink lips and my tongue went right to work.

Fuck.

She tasted like the best thing I have even eaten in all my life.

"Oh, God...Nathan..."

Confident that she wasn't going to push me away, I grabbed the edges of her panties and pulled my face away from her pussy long enough to pull them down and out of my way. As soon as she was free of them, I placed a hand on the back of each thigh and pushed her legs wide and open as far as I could. I buried my face in her soaked cunt and my tongue couldn't capture enough of her slick juices.

"Fuck, baby, you taste delicious," I growled between strokes of my tongue.

"That feels so good..." she cooed, and I wanted to crow.

"Yeah?"

"Yes...oh, God..."

My face was becoming drenched but all that did was make my dick harder than steel. My ego pushed aside the glaring fact that she's been without sex for two years and basked in our talents. I wasn't going to let logic and facts take away from this moment.

I slid a finger inside her pussy as I nibbled on that sensitive button of hers, and fuck me running, she was tight. I really had plans on fucking her all night long, but we'd probably only get three times in at the most. She was going to be sore, and I was going to do my best to make her sore.

A second finger went in and her hands tightened in my hair. I curled them inward and the second I felt the difference in texture, I played with her while making sure my tongue was licking her everywhere.

"I'm going to cum, Nathan," she choked out. "Oh, God...I'm..." I worked her pussy and clit until my name shattered inside the room, and only when her cunt was pulsating around my fingers, did I stop.

I stood up while Andie was catching her breath and I threw off my clothes in record time. Grabbing my pants before they hit the floor, I pulled out my wallet and grabbed the condom that was inside. I had an entire box in the bathroom, but fuck that if I was taking all that time to walk over there and get them. Not right now, at any rate.

I rolled the condom on and grabbed for Andie as I sat down. I straddle her over dick, and still lethargic from her release she had trouble holding on.

I ripped her blouse open, promising to replace it, and when Andie was finally coming to her senses, I said, "I want you to ride me, baby."

"Nathan..." she moaned.

I let the ripped fabric of her blouse hang loose around her as I reached back and unclipped her bra. It was one of those cute ones without straps, so the second I unclipped it, it had fallen on the floor to join my discarded clothing.

Fuck, her tits were magnificent.

I leaned in and took one nipple in my mouth as my hand tightened on her hip. Andie's arms wrapped around the back of my head, and she held me there as I feasted on her heavy, round tits. I was never going to get enough of this woman. I knew it like I knew my own name and I haven't even slid into her pussy yet.

I pulled away from her tit and looked into her dazed brown eyes. "Ride my cock, baby."

"Nathan…"

"Reach down, take my cock, and slide it into that tight, wet pussy, baby." She balanced on her knees and did exactly what I had requested. But when she wrapped her hand around my dick, she froze. "What's wrong?"

Her brown eyes widened. "Nathan, I don't think it's going to fit," she mumbled quietly, and if I weren't dying to get inside her, I'd be basking in this moment, but sliding inside her was the priority here.

"It'll fit, Andrea," I assured her. "Your pussy is so fucking wet, baby, it's going to slide right in." I was lying. It was going to be a struggle, but I could possibly die if she changed her mind right now.

Seriously.

Die.

I watched her take a deep breath and I couldn't stop the groan as she positioned herself over my cock and began to slide down.

I was never going to let this fucking woman leave my bedroom.

"Oh, God…" she hissed. "Oh, oh…."

I held her hips firmly as I told her, "You got this, baby. Ride that cock, Andrea."

"It's so fucking big," she whimpered, and I was going to propose in the fucking morning.

"You can take it," I prayed. "Show me how well you can take my cock."

Andie grabbed onto my shoulders, and after the most agonizing seconds of my life, she finally started riding my dick. Slow at first, but soon, Andie was bouncing on my hard dick like she's been doing it for fucking years.

"Oh, God…Nathan…yes…"

My fingers dug into her hips. "Take that cock, baby," I grunted. "Take what you need." After all, I wasn't the one who's gone two years without sex. I had her on my lap because this was about her, not me. Next time will be about me and the third time will be about *us.*

"You feel so good…" she panted out and this fucking woman was great for my ego. "I'm going to cum al…already…"

I laid back and looked up at her as she really started chasing her high. Andie had her hands flat on my chest as she worked her hips over my dick, making me ready to explode. And because I was about to shoot off, I reached in between our bodies and started playing with her clit. "Cum for me, baby."

The most beautiful sight in the world was watching Andrea throw her head back, scream my fucking name, and cum all over me. Her pussy clamped down on my cock and it was over for me. I shot into the condom and it was the first time in my life I resented having to wear one.

"Nathan…" she moaned before collapsing on my chest, and we stayed like that until my dick softened completely and I had to get rid of the condom.

After rolling her over, I walked to the bathroom to discard the condom and pull out the box I had in there. Walking back into the bedroom, box of condoms in hand, Andrea was laying across my bed on her stomach, seemingly passed out.

I set the box on the nightstand and crawled over her body, kissing my way up her naked form. When I got to her ear, I whispered, "Already out for the count?"

And I laughed when she came back with, "Nope. Just ready for position number two."

Feeling her beneath, I knew I wasn't going to get any sleep tonight.

I knew this.

But then neither was she.

CHAPTER 17

Andrea ~

Pretty sure I was in trouble.

It was Sunday afternoon, and Grant wasn't due home for a few more hours yet, so I came over to Rachel's to spill all the gossip. Charlie had taken their kids, Sarah and Mark, to visits with their grandparents on Charlie's side, and thank God. After spending Friday night, Saturday, Saturday night, and Sunday morning being dicked down by a very impressive penis and the equally impressive man attached to it, I needed to talk to her.

Pronto.

We were sitting outside on the back patio, the weather warm but not unbearable. The iced tea wasn't very icy anymore, but we had more important matters to discuss.

"Wow."

"You have no idea," I exhaled. "I can barely walk, Rach."

"Well, I guess it stands to reason," she said supportively. "He's a big guy. It's expected the equipment would be big, too."

I let out a deep sigh. "It's not just his equipment, Rach," I admitted. "I really like him. He's not at all what I imagined a professional athlete to be, you know." She smiled softly. "And he adores Grant," I added. "What more could I ask for?"

"And you're freaking out why, exactly?"

"Fear of too good to be true?" I wasn't exactly sure why I was anxious about it all, other than the fact that I could seriously see myself getting caught up in Nathan's wave and drowning beneath it.

"Andie, babe, you've always known you were going to have to get back out there again," Rachel pointed out. "And because life is a sadistic sonofabitch, you also knew there could be some hits and misses. Dating is effin' brutal, woman."

I laughed. "Thanks. I feel so much better."

Rachel gave me a lopsided grin. "All I'm saying is to just enjoy Nathan," she advised. "If it works out, great. If it doesn't, it's not the end of the world." She was essentially repeating the same thing I had said to Steven.

"I just never…I'm not sure how I feel about my feelings," I confessed.

She cocked her head. "What do you mean?"

"I really like Nathan," I repeated. "And I wasn't expecting to."

It was so hard to put into words. I was over Steven, I really was. I didn't have any farfetched fantasies that we'd get back together or any pockets of doubt over our divorce. Sure, we got along now, but things had been horrible the year before I finally felt like I had to divorce him. He had been awful and had handled Grant's health condition all wrong. The ugliness was something that I'd never be able to forgive, never mind forget. That alone was enough for me to know that I was over Steven.

Liking someone new felt scary and like another step. Sex with someone else had been another step but *liking* them wasn't just another step; it was a *big* step.

"I just don't want to confuse sex with something more," I told her. "I like him, and this weekend was damn near magical, but…I'm kind of upset with myself that I'm feeling more about this weekend than I should."

"According to who?" she asked not unkindly.

"I don't want to rush it-rush *myself*," I said.

Rachel took a drink of her watered-down iced tea before saying, "Andie, Charlie chased me for months after I called him an idiot." I couldn't stop my smile. It really was a sweet story. Well, if you took out Rachel storming the building, and Rachel causing a scene, and Rachel calling Charlie an idiot. Seriously, if you took out the rage and drama, it really was a sweet story. "Love at first sight *does* exist."

"I'm not saying it doesn't," I countered. "I'm just not ready to crash and burn just yet."

"And you're positive you will?"

"No," I admitted. "But I had concerns, even when I thought I could accept this for a casual fling. Now that I'm finding that I actually like the man…" I shrugged a shoulder. "Maybe I'm just a little gun shy."

"Don't beat yourself up too badly about it, Andie," she said. "It's only been two years since things with Steven officially ended. Maybe you just need to tell Nathan that you need to go slow."

"It's a little too late for that, don't you think?" I deadpanned. "I spent the past two nights naked in his bed."

"Sex and love are two very different things, babe," she replied. "Keep banging the god, but maybe the quality time can run slower."

"What do you mean?"

"Well, for instance, when he comes over to see Grant, then do what you've been doing and make yourself scarce while they spend time together," she suggested. "Don't turn it into some kind of family picture quality time." I could see where she was going with this. "Don't meet his family or introduce him to yours for a few more weeks or a couple of months. That kind of thing."

"So, keep it a secret?"

Rachel shook her head. "Not necessarily a secret, just don't place so much importance on him so soon. If you have errands to run during the weekends, then run them. Don't put them on hold to be with him. Actions speak louder than words, and if you're rearranging your life to be with him, that's telling, Andie. If you need to take it slow, explain that to him," she advised again. "You said you guys talked a lot this weekend, so now that he knows a little more about what you and Steven went through, I'm betting he'll understand wanting to take it slow versus getting offended."

Everything she was saying was making sense, but I still somehow felt stupid for some reason. Like I was running headfirst into a brick wall because I didn't have the sense to open my eyes.

"Oh, not trying to change the subject, because believe me when I say I definitely need more advice, but Justin is introducing a couple of new items to the menu and he asked me to stop by on Wednesday and be a guinea pig. Wanna go with me?"

Her head reared back. "Are you kidding? Free food and booze? Hell yeah, I want to go with you."

I took a drink of my watery tea and smiled. "Charlie won't mind you getting tanked on a Wednesday afternoon?"

She pfft'ed. "Please," she drawled out. "He'll drop the kids off with his parents and take total advantage of me."

I cocked my head. "You have to be drunk for him to take advantage of you?"

She grinned. "Not at all. But the freak flags start to fly in the bedroom when I've been drinking," she joked, only I didn't think she was entirely joking. She and Charlie were nauseatingly in love. I had no doubt they still got the handcuffs out all these years later.

And I wanted that.

I'd had it before Steven had lost his shit and it was something that I wanted again. Not with Steven, but with someone who would adore me just as much as I adored him.

"What are you going to do with Grant?" she asked.

"Steven's parents were clamoring to spend some more time with him before school started," I replied. "So, they're taking him for a movie marathon at the cineplex."

Rachel's grin widened. "Well, since you'll have to be sober when they take him back home, I'll take one for the team and flavor the drinks while you flavor the food."

I laughed. "You're a true friend, Rachel Filmore," I teased. "I don't know what I'd do without you."

"Right?" she said, taking credit for the compliment.

Before I could say anything, my phone chimed and there was no way to ignore the butterflies that erupted in the pit of my stomach.

Nathan: *Thinking of u*

Me: *Good thoughts I hope*

I was so bad at this that I didn't even know what to write back.

Nathan: *Always*

Me: *(smiling emoji)*

"Dude, you got it bad." I looked up at Rachel. "It's all over your face, babe."

I let out a quiet sigh. "Yeah, I suppose I do," I admitted.

Nathan Hayes was definitely the curve ball I hadn't seen coming, and he was definitely better at playing the game than I was.

CHAPTER 18

Nathan ~

Pretty sure I was in trouble.

It's been over two weeks of Andie spending every weekend with me and I was falling fast. Hell, not falling at all. I was pretty sure I've already fallen.

"So, you still haven't met the ex-husband yet?" Sayer's voice came over the phone. Me, him, and Gideon were all on a call together because I needed advice and a little support.

"No, I haven't," I told him. "She wants to take things slow."

While that first weekend had been phenomenal, the following weekend she had told me she had wanted to take things slow. No meeting the parents or anything like that. Andie had admitted to being gun shy and I really couldn't blame her. Two years was two years, but two years were only two years when you considered how long she and Steven had been together and Grant.

So, I got it. I really did.

But it still sucked.

"Think he'll get jealous," Gideon asked.

"I don't think so," I told him. "From what she's told me, he was the one to move on first."

Sayer snorted and I winced. "Yeah, because that matters," he scoffed. His wife's ex-husband had started dating almost immediately after he had divorced Monroe, but that hadn't stopped Thomas from losing his shit when Monroe had started dating Sayer.

"Okay. Point made," I conceded.

"And when are you going to tell Mom," Gideon cut back in. "You saw what she did to Sayer when she found out he'd been after Monroe for a while already and hadn't said anything."

This time Sayer winced. "Yeah," he grumbled. "It wasn't pretty."

Like I had told Andie, though she hadn't believed me, Louise Hayes was that meddling old woman, who had too much time on her hands, but had a temper that could make her grown sons run for cover. She believed our love lives were her business and we'd better not tell her any different. The woman wanted a score of grandkids and she wasn't letting up until she got them.

"I'll tell her soon," I promised. "But you know if I tell her now, the first thing she's going to want to do is meet Andie and Grant. Andie's not ready for Louise Hayes."

"Is anybody?" Sayer deadpanned.

"Hey, fucker," Gideon barked. "That's our mother you're talking about."

"Yeah, and our mother is certifiable, Gid," Sayer barked back. "And don't act like you don't know this."

"Love her to death, but she is insane," I added, siding with Sayer.

"I'll kill you both," Gideon threatened.

"I don't hear you saying we're wrong, though," Sayer fired back.

Gideon hung up on us.

I chuckled as Sayer shook his head. "He's in denial."

"No," I argued. "He's got no choice but to be a part of Mom's madness since he works with Dad."

"Or it could just be that middle-child syndrome he suffers from."

"That, too," I agreed.

"So, is it love?" Sayer asked, changing topics.

"I think it is, Say," I told him truthfully. "I've never felt this way before." Sayer was a great big brother and wasn't as moody as Gideon, so it was easier to talk to him. "She…Andie fucking *dazzles* me, Say."

"Dazzles?" he choked out. "Okay, that's a little too vaginal for me." Then the fucker hung up on me.

So much for being a great big bother.

The asshole.

Before I could call him back and let him know that he was an asshole, in case he was unaware, my doorbell rang. It was programmed through the regular elevator, and if someone was visiting me, they had to push the penthouse button in the elevator to ring me. However, there were only two people who used it and that was Andie and Grant. My parents, brothers, and Sergio used the penthouse elevator whenever they visited. That made me realize I was going to have to give Andie a copy of the penthouse elevator key and see if I could get a third made for Grant.

I walked out into the guest foyer and hit the accept button on the panel near the elevator doors. I knew it could only be Andie or Grant.

And I was right.

Grant came strolling out of the elevator with a big grin on his face and it made my chest ache with happiness. The kid has been on cloud nine ever since his parents told him he'd be going to a live football game. Season opener, no less.

"What's up, kiddo," I said, fist bumping him.

His green eyes looked up at me. "Are you busy?"

"Not too busy for you," I said, telling him the absolute truth. "Wanna come inside?" Grant nodded and we walked into my place. "Want something to eat? Drink?"

"I could use a drink," he replied, and I chuckled at how grown he sounded. Sometimes he sounded just like what an eight-year-old should sound like, and at other times, he sounded like a grown man.

I grabbed him a juice pouch (I started keeping some in my fridge once he started coming over more) and grabbed myself a water before meeting him in the living room.

"What brings you by?" It was Thursday afternoon, and I knew he'd be going off with his dad in a couple of hours, or so.

"Mom's in the zone, so I thought I'd come hang out with you a bit before she has to take me to Dad's."

"Editing or writing?"

"Writing, I think."

I nodded. "So, what's up?"

"Are you dating my Mom?" And thank God I hadn't taken a drink of my water yet or else it would have sprayed everywhere.

"Uh...what?"

"Do you like my Mom? Like, to be her boyfriend?"

Holy fuck.

"Uh...why do you ask?"

"Because whenever you come over, I catch you looking at her like you like her," he said, flooring the fuck out of me.

"I do?"

Grant nodded. "Yeah, you do." Before I could think of a response, he added, "It's okay if you like her. She's nice."

I looked at this kid who owned my heart, and hearing him champion his mother, telling me she was nice, I knew I didn't want to lie to him. He'd never have any respect for me if I did and he was old enough to remember me lying to him if he ever found out the truth.

"Yes, Grant," I told him, hoping I wasn't making a mistake. "I like your mom very much. She's very nice, and pretty, and neat." *Neat?*

He looked at me a long hard minute before saying, "I think she likes you, too."

"What makes you say that?"

"She's happy all the time now," he explained, and I was ready to marry her and adopt him by the end of the week. Sure, Steven might have some objections to adopting his only son but that was a problem for a later date.

"How would you feel if she was my girlfriend?" I was okay with admitting I liked his mother, but I wasn't so clueless as to say more than I should without talking to Andie and/or Steven first.

"That'd be okay with me," he said. "Dad has girlfriends sometimes, and it's what grownup people do, right?"

"Well, I wouldn't be your Mom's sometimes boyfriend," I tried to explain. "I really like your Mom, so I'd be her forever boyfriend." *Forever boyfriend?* Christ, was I fucking this up?

Grant cocked his little eight-year-old head at me, and fucking killed me when he said, "That'd be okay as long as you don't make her cry. My dad made her cry a lot when I was little, and I didn't like it."

I knew there were going to be days when I made Andie cry because I was a man and us men were fucking super stupid sometimes, but it'd never be intentional. However, Grant was too young to explain that to. So, instead, I told him, "I will do my best to never make your mom sad, Grant. You have my word."

"And you and my Dad will be friends, too, right?"

And do you know how I knew it was over for me?

Because I looked this kid in the eyes and said, "Absolutely."

CHAPTER 19

Andrea ~

You have got to be kidding me.

It was late Friday afternoon, and Justin was about to get ready for the dinner and night crowds. He was offering his new dishes and drinks tonight and I had stopped by to wish him luck. Rachel and I had given all three dishes the thumbs up and most of the new drink concoctions, except for the Take A Guess disaster he had served up.

It had tasted like ass.

That hadn't been washed in days.

But after making myself at home at the bar and abusing my perks for free appetizers and a drink, my phone has rung, and since it had been Steven's name that had flashed across the screen, of course, I had answered, and now I was sitting down, stunned at what he was saying.

"Are you...what?"

"Look, I'm not mad," Steven said. "You've been completely honest about what's been going on, Andie. I just would have liked a little heads-up that Grant knew you were dating Nathan. I felt kind of blindsided and hadn't really known how to respond."

Answering the phone, Steven had told me that this morning, over breakfast, Grant had told him that I was dating Nathan. Steven being a real estate agent, he has always been able to set his own hours, so he always took Fridays off, even if that meant he had to put in extra hours Monday through Friday. It was something we both did. We worked our asses off on the days we didn't have Grant, so that we could have more free time on the days we did have with him. We also got along well enough that if we ever needed to trade days or pick up/drop off times, we could.

"Steven, I never told Grant I was dating Nathan," I told him. There had to be some mistake or Grant was just doing some wishful thinking and Steven misunderstood. "What...what did he say, exactly?"

There were a few seconds of silence, but there was no mistaking Steven's tone when he asked, "You never told Grant you were dating Nathan?"

"No," I replied. "I'd never do that without talking to you first. If…if it's serious enough to tell Grant about it, then it's serious enough to talk to you about it and discuss what it could mean."

"He said Nathan told him that he liked you and asked him if it was okay if he was your boyfriend." *What?* "I…I just assumed you guys had discussed it all together."

"An…and when did Nathan tell him this? Do you know? Did he say?"

"I did ask, and Grant said Nathan told him yesterday afternoon," he said. "Did Grant visit Nathan yesterday?"

My stomach dipped with realization. "Yeah," I mumbled into the phone. "He went to visit him at his place a couple of hours before I dropped him off with you."

"And Nathan didn't say anything to you about it?"

"No." Steven remained silent, so I went on to explain. "When I got back from dropping Grant off, Nathan had sent me a text that a water line had busted in his parents' backyard. He'd gone over there to help out. I…I worked all Thursday evening, and I'd woken up to a text his morning that he'd see me today. The text had come in at around midnight, so I assumed he stayed to help fix the water line, or…something."

"And this morning?"

"I was working all morning, final edits and stuff, and…"

"And?"

"Well, he sent me another text telling me he was going to go check on his parents water line again, just to double check in the light of day that it was fixed, and I got back to work." It was like a bad movie where everything was going wrong, but Nathan could still have picked up the phone or sent me a text that we needed to talk. Something. *Anything.*

"Where are you now?"

"Justin's got some new items on the menu tonight, and so I stopped by to wish him luck," I replied. "I'm at the bar."

"And no calls or texts from Nathan?"

"Just a text earlier that he'll stop by tonight," I muttered, feeling more and more foolish by the second. How could he have a conversation like that with my son, after telling him I wanted to take things slow, and not tell me about it? Not make the time to tell me about it?

"Look, Andie," Steven started, and I knew that tone. However, I wasn't sure I didn't deserve whatever he was about to say to me. "I've done my best to respect you and your choices. It's my fault we're divorce, and I own that. I've swallowed that bitter pill and it sits like a rock in the pit of my stomach every fucking day. However, part of taking responsibility for what I've done is moving on and allowing you to move on, too. I want you to be happy, Andie. I swear to God, I do. I know there will still be these pockets of nostalgia that will cause some tender aches from time-to-time, but I want us to both be happy. For Grant's sake, if nothing else." I could feel the pressure behind my eyes because I knew where this was going, and I *did* deserve it. "But I am *not* going to stand back and let your boyfriend, or *any* of your boyfriends should this thing with Nathan not work out, overstep and start making decisions that affect Grant's life."

"I know," I muttered pathetically, but Steven wasn't feeling charitable at the obvious distress in my voice.

"He has been overstepping since the very beginning and I won't stand for it any longer, Andie," Steven continued. "Grant is *our* son. Married or divorced, he is *ours*. And even if you were to marry Nathan tomorrow, Grant is still *our* son. I am not an absent father and you are not a neglectful mother. Nathan fucking Hayes does not need to step into our dynamic and turn it upside down. And he doesn't get to start deciding what is best for Grant."

"I know, Steven," I repeated because I did know. Nathan overstepped in a way he never should have.

"When are you going home from the bar?"

"Uh...now," I replied, still...shocked. "Uh...I just...let me tell Justin goodbye and...and I'll head home."

"Text me when you get there and Grant and I will head over," he said. "We can talk to him together and...see what we're dealing with."

"O...okay."

"Okay."

"Steven?"

"What, Andie?"

"I'm sorry," I said softly. "I...I never would...I didn't mean for this to...to happen. I-"

"Andrea, you didn't do anything wrong, except trust someone a little too quickly, maybe," he graciously replied. "I'm not mad at you. There's only one person I blame for this clusterfuck, and it's not you."

"I'll see you when I get home," I said simply. I didn't want to get into *that* conversation until I knew what I was dealing with. There was a good chance that Nathan would win a physical altercation between him and Steven since he was taller and more muscular, but Steven wasn't soft, either. Steven would give as good as he got if it ever came down to that.

After telling Justin I had to go home, I had driven home in a bit of a fog. I probably hadn't been in the condition to drive, but I had made it home safely and hadn't mowed anyone else down in the process.

I had texted Steven and he and Grant had come over immediately. Together, we had asked him about his conversation with Nathan, and while Grant hadn't thought anything of it, with every word out of his mouth I had become angrier and angrier.

The second Grant had asked him if we were dating, Nathan should have walked him back to my place and let me deal with it. He never should have discussed anything about the nature of our relationship with Grant. Especially, after having made it clear that I had wanted to take things slow. If I didn't want our parents know just yet, it should have been easy to deduce that I hadn't been ready to let Grant know just yet, either.

When Grant was done telling us about his conversation with Nathan, I had racked my brain with the best way to explain how Nathan and I were just friends, because though that was a lie, moving forward, we *were* going to be just friends.

I hated lying to Grant, but better than let him believe he messed things up between me and Nathan. There was no way I was going to let Grant think he broke us up.

The only person who had broken us up was Nathan.

I was furious, but I couldn't deny how disappointed I was, either. I had let my guard down and trusted the wrong man *again*.

How could I have been so stupid?

CHAPTER 20

Nathan ~

You have got to be kidding me.

Andrea hadn't been answering my texts all afternoon, and while I knew she had a tendency to get absorbed in her work, she usually sent a text when she took a break. She hasn't replied to a single text since this morning, and I missed her terribly.

Last night had been a fucking disaster when Sayer had called me to tell me the water line in Mom and Dad's backyard had busted. Now while my dad and Gideon were perfectly capable of handling the issue, since they were the construction engineers in the family, Sayer and I didn't get down like that. Dad was sixty-five, and while still in good shape, he had three strong, young sons for the hard shit.

Sayer and I had arrived just as Gideon had finished digging up the grass over the break, and even though it was already heading towards darkness, Dad had brought out a flood light from the shed and we had worked by that light alone. Gideon had run to the hardware store before it had closed and had gotten everything we might need, and then some.

After working close to ten, we had fixed it, and by the time Mom had fed us a very late dinner, it had been midnight by the time I had gotten back home. I had fired off a text to Andie with the small hope that she might still be up, but when she hadn't responded, I had showered and had fallen out.

This morning I had woken up to a text from Gideon telling me that he and Sayer were heading over to Mom and Dad's to double check our handiwork. I, too, had gone over this morning in case our work by flood light had sucked.

After checking on everything, Mom had insisted on a big breakfast for us all, and since Dad would kick our asses if we were to upset his wife, we had all stayed and had eaten breakfast. Even Sayer had stayed, knowing it was going to make him late to the firehouse. But since everyone at the firehouse has met

Louise Hayes, even his chief would make this one allowance.

Again, Mom was batshit crazy and everyone knew it but Gideon.

So, not having seen Andie since the other day, and her not returning my texts or answering my calls, I came downstairs to her condo to see if she was okay. What I hadn't expected to see was an older version of Grant answering her fucking door.

And I certainly hadn't expected the steel in his voice when he asked, "Can I help you?"

Now, I wasn't a complete idiot. This was obviously Steven, Grant's dad and Andie's ex. It was uncanny how much Grant looked like him, but then me, Sayer, and Gideon all looked like Dad. None of us had inherited anything from Mom.

I reined in my immediate reaction to puff my chest out, and said, "Is Andie home?"

Steven surprised me when he shut the door behind him, forcing me to have to take a step back out into the hallway. I was taller than he was by about three inches, or so and I also filled out a little more than was his stature, but none of that really mattered. This man was the father of Andie's child and the only man she's ever pledged to spend her entire life with. Right now, he was more important than whatever it was that we were beginning to build between us.

"I'm Steven Hansen," he started. "I'm Grant's father and Andrea's ex-husband."

I arched a brow coolly. "I gathered as much."

"Are you sure?"

"Meaning?"

"Well, it seems to me as you if you like to pretend that I don't exist," he replied smoothly. But then his tone took on a hard edge when he added, "But I do."

"Not sure what you mean by that, but I'm very well aware that you exist," I told him. "Grant and Andie talk about you all the time."

"Then, maybe, you can answer something for me," he smirked, and I was starting to really not like the man. He looked like he had an ace up his sleeve that he was dying to play.

"Oh, yeah? What's that?"

"Why would you take it upon yourself, when Grant has two very involved parents, to tell an eight-year-old boy how you like his mother when she specifically asked you to take things slow?"

My heart skipped before beginning to beat painfully in my chest.

How could I have forgotten about that?

I donned my best poker face. "With all due respect, that's a conversation that needs to be had between me and Andie."

"It's a conversation that should have been had with Andie *before* you had taken it upon yourself to have it with Grant," he shot back.

"Whatever you think happened, it didn't happen that way," I replied, hating that I had to explain myself to this man.

This time, he was the one who arched a brow. "Really? Because the way we heard it was that Grant asked you if you were dating his mother, and instead of sending back home to have that conversation with Andie or calling Andie to tell him Grant was asking those important questions, you just went on to talk to him about something that Andie informed you she was sensitive about." The fucker shook his head. "Are you telling me that's not how it happened?"

"Where's Andie?" I asked. I wasn't saying the man didn't have the right to be annoyed with me, but this was something between me, Andie, and Grant.

"She's inside with Grant trying to answer any questions he might have about what's going on between the two of you," he replied, and I immediately felt like everything was crashing down all around me. "Why the hell do you think I'm answering her door?"

"Because you're a dick?" The words came flying out, but I wasn't going to apologize for them. My soul felt a little chaotic, and I wasn't sure if I could control my emotions right now.

Steven smirked. "Not denying that, but that's not why," he said. "She asked me to please answer the door, because suspecting it might be you, she's pissed the fuck off and she's trying to hide it from Grant. So, better for me to answer the door and deal with you, than chance her losing her shit in front of her son." I clenched my jaw. "Do you think she wants Grant to witness a fight between the two of you?"

"So, I take it I'm not allowed inside?"

He surprised me again when he shook his head. "Actually, you're more than welcome to come inside," he said. "But trust me when I tell you that's not actually a good thing."

Steven turned back to open the door and I following him inside. Whether or not shit was going to go sideways, I wasn't a coward. I had no problem admitting when I was wrong. However, I didn't feel like I was. I might have handled Grant's questioning wrong, but my intentions hadn't been bad. I hadn't wanted to lie to the kid and my feelings for Andie were the real thing. We were going to have to tell Grant the truth at some point.

I followed Steven into the living room and Andie was sitting on the couch with Grant. When Grant saw me, he smiled and said, "Hi, Nate."

"Hi, Kiddo."

"Did you meet my dad?"

I smiled a forced smile. "Yeah, I did."

Steven and I stood almost next to each other behind the couch while Grant rambled on. "I was just telling my mom how you said you wanted to be her forever boyfriend. That's okay, right?"

The tension in the room was thick but everyone was doing their best not to let it touch Grant. "Of course, it's okay," I told him. "But...I probably should have told that myself, yeah?"

He chewed on his lower lip a bit and I hated putting that look on his face. "Well, I told my dad and he said I needed to tell my mom, so she can decide if she wants to be your forever girlfriend."

Fuck it.

I walked around the couch and sat next to Grant. "Your dad is right," I told him. "It *is* up to your Mom, and I should have asked her first, instead of saying anything."

"But you guys can still be friends, right?"

My heart dropped.

"Uh, of course," I said. I had to clear my throat for a second. "It's important to be friends."

Grant looked like he was giving it some thought, then gave a small nod. "Well, Mom says you guys are just friends, but that's fine because you'll be able to find another forever girlfriend."

And then my saving grace came from the last place I would have ever expected.

"Hey, bud," Steven said, calling to Grant's attention," why don't we get going before it gets too late for Friday Fries."

Grant's face lit up. "Okay." He went and hugged Andie before turning around to hug me. "I gotta go," he said. "It's time for Friday Fries." I had no idea what that was, but I smiled anyway.

"Call me if you need anything, Andie," Steven said before grabbing Grant and taking off. "Nice meeting you, Nathan," he lied as the door shut behind him and Grant.

Fucking asshole.

CHAPTER 21

Andrea ~

One of the hardest things to do was listen when you were in the right.

And pissed off.

When I had heard the knock on the door, I'd known it was probably Nathan. Rachel and my parents always texted when they were going to stop by. Especially, on the weekends because they knew that's when I put in my most work hours. But because I had been upset and angry, I had asked Steven to answer the door because I hadn't been able to trust that my emotions wouldn't get the better of me. This entire thing was a mess, and I wasn't going to add to it by fighting with Nathan in front of Grant and Steven.

And now Steven and Grant were gone, leaving me alone with Nathan, and I. Was. Pissed.

"Andie-"

"Don't, Nathan," I said, interrupting him, and it was a miracle I could get those two little words out with how clenched my teeth were.

"I was going to tell you," he said, ignoring my command. "But it slipped my mind with that mess at my parents last night. I-"

"There never should have been anything to tell me," I snapped, my composure lost. "The second Grant asked you if we were dating, you should have walked him back home, so we could have that conversation together."

"I didn't tell him we were dating, though," he argued. "I just told him I liked you."

I scoffed.

Was he really so clueless?

"You're Nathan Hayes," I reminded him incredulously. "You tell a little boy, whose entire life is sports, that you like his mom, and you don't think he's going to get excited and hopeful?" I shook my head. "Breaking up with you isn't like breaking up with some unassuming insurance salesman, Nate. Grant adores you. He adored you, even before we met, because you represent

83

everything that he loves in life. What in the hell did you think he would think if you told him you liked his mother?"

"I was blindsided, okay?" he said, trying to excuse his error in judgement. "But I never told him we were dating. I just-"

"But you might as well have," I argued. "A famous professional baseball player tells him that he like his mother and Grant couldn't see past the excitement long enough to understand the difference. He's eight-years-old, Nate, not twenty-eight."

"Look-"

"From the beginning, you have been coming into our lives with all the finesse of a wrecking ball," I continued. "I've had to tell you, *several times*, to back off when it came to Grant and you've completely disrespected my wishes." He went to open his mouth, but I didn't stop. "I've been completely honest with you about being gun shy and wanting to take things slow and why. I have made myself as clear as can be with my situation and my demons and you just don't care."

"That's not fair!" he exploded. "How can you say I don't care? Because of one little fuck-up?"

"One little fuck-up? Are you serious?" I seethed. "This wasn't just one little fuck-up, Nathan. Disrespecting my wishes is not some minor offense that can be waved away. Especially, when it involves my son."

Nathan crossed his arms over his chest. "Is that you talking or your ex-husband?" he asked coolly, and I could feel my entire body lock up.

"Excuse me?"

"I mean, he is your ex, right? Because I gotta tell you, it sure doesn't seem that way with all the liberties he takes and how chummy the two of you are."

If I thought I was seething before, that was nothing compared to the rage boiling in my veins right now. "Chummy?"

"Yeah, chummy," he repeated. "It seems like all your objections are his objections."

"Just because you and your ex-wife can't get along for the sake of your children, doesn't mean me and Steven aren't allowed to be friends," I snapped.

Nathan's arms dropped to his side and confusion marred his perfect face. He shook his head, and his forehead furrowed as he looked at me. "What are you talking about? I don't have an ex-wife or any children."

"Exactly," I snarled. "You stand there, judging the type of relationship I have with Steven, when you have no fucking clue what it's like to be divorce and have to make things work for the sake of your child's happiness." I could feel my nose tingle with the onset of some tears, but I was so livid, I didn't have enough control to stop whatever tears might escape. "Your parents are still happily married, and neither you nor your brothers have ever gone through their own divorce. But you're going to stand there and spout bullshit like you understand what it's like? You're going to comment on mine and

Steven's friendship when you have no idea the pain, regret, and torment we went through to be able to be the friends we are now?" I let out a deep sigh of disgust. "Would you rather we hated each other, and Grant be left to lead a life where his parents used him as a bargaining chip or shattered his innocence with fights and name-calling?"

"Andr-"

"We already wrecked that precious kid's life when we got a divorce, but your ego and insecurities are so fragile, we have to ruin his life some more just so you don't feel threatened?" I shook my head in repugnance and disappointment. "Spoken like a true spoiled athlete who isn't used to the word 'no'."

"Just like I don't know what it's like to be a father or divorced, you don't know what it's like to be a professional athlete, so why don't *you* refrain from judging?"

That was it.

That was all.

No apology for judging something he couldn't possibly understand.

No apology for overstepping again.

Just a small acknowledgment that he may have fucked-up, but it wasn't that big of a fuck-up because he hadn't told Grant we were dating, just that he liked me.

I didn't need this shit.

No matter how much I was beginning to care for Nathan, I didn't need this shit.

I took a deep breath and did the same thing I'd done when my marriage had been falling apart; I did what was best for Grant.

"Look, if you still want to be friends with Grant, I'm fine with that-"

"Are you fucking serious?" Nathan growled, and he looked pissed, but what did he have to be pissed about? I wasn't the one who betrayed his trust.

"If you still want to be friends with Grant-"

"I will always want to be friends with Grant," he interrupted. "But are you seriously breaking up with me over one mistake? No grace period? No second chance? No nothing? It's just over because I fucked up *once?*"

"Once is one time too many if it involves my son," I shot back.

"Oh, for fuck's sake, Andrea," he snapped. "I told Grant I liked you. It's not like I told him it makes you wet when I choke you with my cock-"

And that was my limit.

That was my limit. and it was obvious that Nathan knew it, too, because his blue eyes widened as he abruptly stopped his rant.

The fact that it was true, and that it had been something that I had expressed during the heat of passion, felt like a slap in the face. It was a harsh reminder of all the things I had trusted Nathan with, and proof that I really was stupid with it came to men.

"Get out of my house," I told him. No screaming. No crying. No anything.

"Andrea-"

"Get. Out. Of. My. House," I repeated a little bit more forcefully.

He stared at me for a few tense seconds, then said, "Okay. Maybe we both need to cool down-"

I shook my head. "You don't understand," I interrupted. "I won't object to your friendship with Grant, but I want nothing more to do with you, Nathan."

He quickly stepped towards me. "Andie-"

"Get out of my house, Nathan." He looked like he was going to argue, so I hit him with something I knew he couldn't risk, considering who he was. "Or I will call the police."

His head reared back, like he'd just taken a physical blow. "Andie..."

"Andrea," I corrected, and I didn't utter another word as I watched Nathan take a deep breath before turning around and walking out my front door.

The tears didn't come until around midnight.

CHAPTER 22

Nathan ~

One of the hardest things to do was listen to all the ways you were wrong.

And I *was* wrong.

On so many fucking levels.

I was so fucking wrong that Gideon had even toned down his dickish ways because the asshole was feeling so sorry for me.

"I have to admit, I'm at a bit of a loss here," Sayer mumbled helplessly.

After Andie-or *Andrea*-kicked me out of her condo, I wasn't too proud to admit I had been a fucking mess. I fucked up, and I had fucked up *badly*.

However, the magnitude of my fuck-up hadn't really registered until I had shown up at Sayer's and he hadn't automatically jumped in to defend me or side with me. After I had shared with him the clusterfuck that I found myself in, he had grabbed me a beer, told me to sit down, and had called Gideon. And the fact that he had called Gideon to help with this mess was also telling. Gideon didn't pull his punches. He told you what he thought and why, and you just had to deal with it. If Sayer called Gideon, that meant we were going to need a referee. Gideon was logic and facts while Sayer and I were more prone to reacting emotionally. Sayer from being spoiled as the firstborn, and me from being spoiled as the baby of the family. Gideon…Gideon wasn't spoiled.

"What exactly are you confused about, Say?" Gideon asked. "Nate was a fucking asshole to her."

See?

"I wasn't an asshole, per s-"

Gideon looked like he wanted to deck me. "Dude, instead of just going over there and apologizing for not staying in your lane, you insulted her by downplaying something that's obviously important to her, and then attacked her relationship with her ex-husband," Gideon scoffed. "And as much as Sayer wants to be the supportive big brother, have you fucking learned nothing from his experience?"

"Meaning?" I asked, sounding like a legit brat.

"Meaning Monroe's ex-husband is a total dick," he answered as if I hadn't already known this. "Do you know how much easier Sayer's life would be if Monroe and Thomas got along like Andrea and her ex-husband did? Do you have any idea how much happier Leta would be?" With every question he posed, I felt lower and lower. "You stumble across a great kid, who can outmatch you in sports by the way, and he comes with a hot mother who is a good person but stupid enough to like your dumb ass, and she gets along with her ex, so there's no fucking drama, and what do you do?" When me and Sayer remained silent, he answered his own questioned. "You throw a fucking tantrum because you're Nathaniel fucking Hayes, professional baseball shortstop, America's darling, and you can't possibly imagine that anything wouldn't go your way."

"C'mon, Gid," Sayer interjected. "That's kind of harsh, don-"

"Harsh?" Gideon's brows shot up. "Who has Nate ever had to be responsible for besides himself, in all his life?" Sayer's eyes cut my way. "That's right. *No one.*"

"That's not fair," Sayer said, defending me, though I wasn't sure I deserved it. A lot of what Gideon was saying felt like burning acid in my stomach.

"Do you want to know what's not fair, Say?" Gideon challenged. "If Nate didn't have Mom or Dad looking after him, he had you doing it. And if you weren't around, he had me doing it. All of us, we've always made sure Nate was taken care of because he was the baby. It was our job to look out for him and that is not something that I've ever regretted or resented." Gideon looked back at me. "I love you, Nate. I love you like I would take a bullet for you. I would die for you if that was what needed to be sacrificed. You're my brother." He looked over at Sayer. "I'd do the same for you." Returning those piercing blue eyes back my way, he said, "But never having been responsible for another person, be it sibling, wife, or child, you stood there as the judge, jury, and executioner on Andrea's life and her choices." He shook his head. "Don't you see how fucked-up that is? This woman is still picking up the pieces of a failed marriage while working with her ex-husband the best way she knows how in dealing with the health of their son. And here you come along and tell her your interference in what she's trying to maintain is no big deal. You tell her to get over it because it was just some minor fuck-up in your opinion. That's-"

"Enough!" I couldn't take his truth any longer.

"Is it, though?" he retorted.

"Yes," I hissed. "I hear you, loud and clear, Gid."

"Nate-"

I looked over at Sayer. "It's okay, Say," I told him. "Gideon's not wrong."

"He doesn't need to be a dick about it," Sayer bit out.

Gideon looked over at him. "I'm sorry," he remarked, the sarcasm dripping. "Did you call me over here to cradle his balls while you stroked his dick?"

"Uh, okay," I grimaced. "Can we not talk about my brothers doing *anything* with my dick and balls?"

Sayer shook his head. "Okay, can we get to fixing this instead of placing unnecessary blame? Nate already knows he fucked up. He wouldn't be here if he didn't."

"You fucked with her kid," Gideon said. "You can't fix this."

My head reared back. "Seriously? You're going to actually say that fucked-up shit to me?"

"Because Mom wouldn't lose her shit or end up in jail if anyone fucked with any of us?" Gideon let out a dark chuckle. "They don't call them momma bears for nothing, Nate."

I felt like I was going to throw up.

I was in love with Andie. This mess proved it. I wouldn't be feeling like my life was over if I weren't in love with her. The second I had reduced her concerns to a sordid sex act, I knew I had crossed an unforgivable line. Sure, I'd been swerving outside my lane for a while where she was concerned-as Gideon put it-but that had been crass and uncalled for. Even I knew that.

"I have an idea," Sayer offered. "But I'm not sure you're going to like it."

"What is it?" I wasn't proud. "I'll do anything, Say."

"You're going to have to throw yourself on the sword and talk to the ex," he said.

"What?"

"He's right," Gideon remarked, agreeing with Sayer.

"How do you figure?" While that shitshow earlier could have been worse, I wasn't quite ready to become BFFs with Steven Hansen.

"If he can forgive you for overstepping with their son, then Andrea might be willing to give you the benefit of the doubt. If the one man-who has *no reason* to like you or spare you-is willing to listen to you, then maybe she will, too."

I hated how their jacked-up advice was making sense. The last thing I wanted to do was ask Andie's ex to help me fix my relationship with her, but what else could I do? I just told Sayer I'd do anything to make it right, right?

Fuck, maybe I was a spoiled little shit after all.

"I guess that's still better than the plan I don't have," I grumbled, hating the idea.

Gideon let out a deep sigh and I knew I was exhausting him. He was not a fan of drama. That's why he was always yelling at us when Mom got on him because her theatrics were too much for him sometimes. "Look, Nate, even if she doesn't forgive you, this way, at least you can say you tried everything, right?"

I looked between my two brothers and asked the one question I really didn't want an honest answer to. "Do you think she'll forgive me?"

It was Sayer who delivered the blow. "No, Nate. I don't think she will," he said sadly.

"But if she does," Gideon said, their roles reversed. "If she does, Nate, then you better appreciate that gift for what it is for the rest of your fucking life."

"You think I won't?"

"I think you're finally going to learn the hard way what it's like to be responsible for other people," he replied, back to being the dick.

"I don't even know how to get a hold of Steven," I grumbled.

"You know how to get a hold of Grant, right?" Sayer asked.

"Yeah. We exchanged cell numbers a couple of weeks ago."

"Well, there you go."

I pulled my phone out and sent a text to an eight-year-old, asking him to have his dad-who he thinks I'm friends with now-to call me.

This was going to suck.

But the alternative?

That would suck even more.

CHAPTER 23

Andrea ~

Well, I wasn't expecting this.

Steven walked past me into the living room, no Grant in sight.

"Where's Grant? With your parents?"

He eyed me and blurted out sadly, "You look like crap, Andie."

"Geez, thanks," I grumbled. "You sure know how to flatter a lady." The jerk grinned and I just shook my head.

Some days, I didn't know how to take him. At times, we felt like old friends, and at other times, we could seem like distant strangers. I suppose it could just be a matter of mood swings or good days versus bad days, but I knew that me and Steven were probably always going to be a work in progress. At least, for a few more years.

His face softened when he asked, "Crying all night?"

"This feels really weird talking to you about this, Steven," I replied sardonically.

His grin widened. "Well, it's about to get even weirder."

My eyes narrowed. "What do you mean? And where's Grant?" I asked again.

Steven's green eyes regarded me closely as he informed me, "He's upstairs with Nathan."

My stomach rolled.

"What?"

He threw his hands up in surrender. "Calm down-"

"Then you better get to talking, Steven," I bit out.

"Last night, Nathan texted Grant asking him to ask me to call him," he said, throwing me into complete shock.

"What?!" I screeched.

"Andie, hear me out," he implored. "Just…hear me out, and…and if you still want nothing to do with Nathan, I'll support you completely. Okay?" I

91

was staring at my ex-husband as I was trying to accept that he was here on Nathan's behalf.

This was too weird by half.

I took a deep breath and decided to ride this train wreck until it crashed. "Okay."

"It took me a long while to finally pick up the phone and call Nathan back," he began. "It sort of felt like…I was betraying you, or something. But then…"

"But then?"

His face looked so emotionally sincere, I almost choked up. "But then I remembered what it felt like to lose you. His call took me back to those desperate memories where I knew I had fucked up beyond what I could repair. I felt for the man, and so I called him."

"Steven…" I didn't really know what to say, but to say I was emotionally confused was a super understatement.

"So, I called him, and he asked if I could meet him somewhere or if he could stop by. I called my parents and asked if they could watch Grant for a bit, and after dropping him off, I met Nathan at Just One More Cup." Just One More Cup was a café that was opened around the clock. The entire world didn't work banker hours and Just One More Cup understood this.

"And?"

"First, he owned up to overstepping, but not just with telling Grant he was interested in you," he continued. "He apologized for not staying in his lane." Steven chuckled. "Those were his words, not mine." I thought about that and it was probably a very accurate description of Nathan's behavior since the first night we met. "After that, he apologized for not taking the time to understand something he's never experienced. He admitted to only seeing everything through the eyes of a person who'd never had the kind of responsibilities you and I had."

"Okay, so he apologized and explained why he was irresponsible and an asshole, but that still doesn't explain why you're here on his behalf, Steven," I told him. "And quite frankly, this is weird, Steven."

He let out a soft chuckle. "I'm very aware, Andrea."

"Okay, so he apologized, admitted to being clueless, and…?"

"And I think the man really cares about you, Andie," he replied. "In fact, I'm pretty sure the man is in love with you."

My heart dropped at hearing him say those words. "What makes you say that?"

"Because he looked like a goddamn mess, Andie," he claimed. "He looked worse than you do right now, and you've been crying your eyes out all night."

"Ha. Ha," I deadpanned.

"I'm serious," he said as he made his way over, put his hands on my shoulders, then rubbed them up and down. "I just know that look, Andrea."

"Why are you doing this, Steven?" Even if everything he was saying was true, I still couldn't reconcile the fact that Steven was here, and he was pleading Nathan's case.

"Because I can tell you I'm sorry, every day for the rest of my life, but those two words mean nothing without any action behind them, Andrea." I felt like I was being pummeled emotionally, good, bad, sad...all of them. "I don't want you to just *hear* how sorry I am, I want you to *know* it. And the only way I can prove how sorry I am for everything I've caused is to do whatever I need to in order to make sure you and Grant are happy. And Nathan was making you happy, Andie."

"But he-"

"Stop," he commanded, his hands sliding into his pockets. "While what Nathan did was reckless, it wasn't malicious. His talk with Grant was ill-advised, but you know he didn't do it to hurt you or Grant."

"But-"

"Andrea, don't make Nathan pay for my mistakes," he said sternly. "You're gun shy, and I understand that. I really do. But ending things this abruptly because of a misunderstanding is a bit extreme, don't you think?"

I thought about that for a few seconds. "The argument got ugly," I said, letting him know there was more to it.

Steven nodded. "I know, Andie," he replied, surprising me again. "Nathan didn't go into details, but he admitted to getting immature and ugly after me and Grant left."

I couldn't stop the quiet tears that came. "I'm scared, Steven," I confessed.

His voice scratched when he said, "I know, Andrea. And I'm so fucking sorry. I'm so fucking sorry I did that to you." He pulled his hands out of his pockets and yanked me into his arms. "I'll support you, no matter what you decide with Nathan, but I really do believe the man loves you. And I just want to see you happy."

"I really care about him, Steven," I admitted. "It's a scary feeling to care about someone like that again."

"I know," he murmured against my hair. "But just hear him out, Andie. Hear him out, and if you don't see what I saw, then I agree, move the hell on. But don't throw the baby out with the bath water because it's easier."

"Did you just call me a coward?" I asked, my voice a watery chuckle.

"Yeah, I'm pretty sure I did," he challenged back.

I pulled out of his arms and looked up at him. "Thank you, Steven."

He smiled down at me. "You're welcome, Andrea." He jerked his head towards the door. "I'm going to go get Grant, and then we'll be on our way. Okay?"

I nodded. "Okay."

Steven kissed me on the top of my head and I just stood there as he walked out of my condo, on his way upstairs to get Grant.

A part of me could admit that Steven was right about my knee-jerk reaction and ending things with Nathan just to protect myself, but I also knew there could be no misunderstanding about the lengths I would go to in order to protect Grant from any more unnecessary heartache.

But then, I suppose I wouldn't be so scared of Nathan Hayes if I weren't already falling in love with him. I wouldn't be so scared if he didn't have the potential to hurt me just as badly as Steven had. And I guess I had to decide if I'd rather be scared than happy.

Easy, right?

And then there was still the fact that we were neighbors, and if Grant and Nathan were going to remain friends, then I wasn't walking away from Nathan free and clear. He was going to be around, and was this something so big that I really couldn't get past it?

Was I going to regret not hearing him out later down the road?

Was I going to regret hearing him out?

And which was going to hurt more?

CHAPTER 24

Nathan ~

Well, I wasn't expecting this.

When Steven had agreed to talk to her for me, I really hadn't expected it to work. Now, while I had prayed for the best, I didn't really think he could pull it off. But the man had done me a solid I wasn't sure I'd ever be able to repay, whether Andie forgave me or not.

After he came back to pick up Grant, he hadn't given me much, other than she had listened to him, though she hadn't said anything about whether or not she was going to give me a second chance. He said she had just thanked him for his efforts, and that was that.

So, when the doorbell had sounded from the public elevator, I had gotten my hopes up way high. However, as I stood in the doorway, looking at her, I was actually afraid to say anything.

Her brows rose a bit. "May I come in?"

Feeling like an idiot, I stepped back and opened the door wider to allow her entrance. "Sure," I muttered.

Andie walked in and made her way to into the middle of the inside foyer. I shut the door as she turned around to face me. She didn't say anything, and I could only stare at her. But to be fair, even if she were speaking, I wasn't sure I'd be able to hear anything over the rush of blood in my hears and the pounding in my chest.

When I couldn't stand it any longer, I said, "I'll do anything."

Her face softened a bit. "I suppose recruiting Steven is kind of proof of that."

"I didn't know what else to do," I admitted. "And I hadn't even been the one to come up with that idea if I'm being honest. My brothers came up with it."

"Your brothers?" She looked surprised.

"Yeah. Uh, after I left yesterday, I went over to Sayer's and Gideon met us there," I told her. "I needed...them."

Andie let out a deeps sigh. "Nathan-"

I rushed up on her and put my hands on her shoulders, not caring if she was going to deck me for touching her. Anyway, it'd be worth it. "I know I fucked up, Andie," I rushed out. "I know I overstepped and acted like a complete dick during our fight, but...fuck, baby, I *swear* to you, I never meant to undermine you or...confuse Grant. I would never do anything to hurt that kid." And that was the God's honest truth. "Grant thinks Steven and I are friends, for fuck's sake." She huffed out a small chuckle. "And I would never do anything to hurt you, Andie. *Never.*"

She grimaced. "Steven pointed out that I may have let my...uh, old ghosts get out of hand yesterday." I pulled her to me, and she let me.

She fucking let me.

I was probably crushing her, but I couldn't think about that right now. "I'm sorry, baby," I whispered against the top of her head. "I'm so fucking sorry, and...I'll do better."

Andrea pulled back, and I let her. Looking up at me, she asked, "Do better?"

I winced. "Gideon may or may not have pointed out to me that I've been a spoiled brat all my life and I could probably benefit from other points of view on life."

"He called you a spoiled brat?"

"He also called me a dumbass," I admitted. "And said something to the effect of how being the baby of the family and America's darling might have contributed to my head being stuck up my ass."

She grinned. "I think I like Gideon."

I smiled back until I realized she hasn't said anything about forgiving me or taking me back. "Want to sit down?"

She nodded. "Yeah, I would."

I led her through the living room and got her settled on the couch. "Would you like anything to drink?"

Andie shook her head. "No, thank you. I just...I just really would like to get this conversation over with."

That did not sound good.

"Uh, okay," I agreed, worried as I took a seat next to her. But then I remembered she had let me hug her. But was that a friend hug? She also hadn't corrected me when I had called her baby, so that was a good thing, right?

I looked into her perfect brown eyes. "So, tell me what I have to do, Andrea," I said. "Tell me what to do, and I'll do it."

"What if you're not up to the task?" she asked.

That got me curious. "What if I am?" Did she forget that I was a retired professional athlete? Competition and excelling were in my blood.

"Okay," she said, regarding me with doubt all over her pretty face. Or maybe that was just my insecurities creeping through.

"What's the task?"

She took a deep breath. "I need you to love Grant like he's your own, but I need you to also *understand* that he's not yours." She suddenly looked tired, and I didn't like that. "I know it's an unfair condition," she went on. "I know it sucks to invest yourself in someone but have no say in the important things. I know that's unfair and…kind of shitty, actually. But…" Andie shrugged her shoulder as if to say, 'oh well', and she wasn't wrong.

That *was* a shitty situation. But then I thought of Sayer and wondered how he dealt with it. But then again, Leta was a teenager with no health issues. It wasn't quite apples and apples. However, I was sure this was something Sayer could help me with if I ever found myself fumbling with it.

"I can do my best," I told her. And for a little more reassurance, I added, "With Sayer having a stepdaughter he absolutely adores, I can always talk to him for advice if I'm struggling."

She didn't comment at first, but then she muttered, "I think you really are going to be more trouble than you're worth, Nathan."

Are going to be?

"Meaning?" I needed it in words. I'd already fucked up epically, so I needed the words.

"Meaning, while you're working on knowing your place, I'll be working on keeping Steven in his, Grant in his, and me in mine," she replied.

Huh?

"What does that mean, Andie?" I asked because I was confused as fuck.

"It means that…if we're going to do this, then we all have a lot to learn," she grumbled, and I wasn't sure if her words were a positive or a negative because the woman did not look happy.

"So…am I forgiven?" *Fuck it.* I might as well ask straight-out because I was still confused.

She let out a choked laugh. "Yes, Nat-*oh, oomph-*" Andrea was perched on my lap before she could say anything more.

"You're not fucking with me, are you?"

She shook her head. "I was scared, Nate," she confessed. "That's it. That's all. While you did mess up big time, I let fear dictate how I handled it. I let fear lead in my reaction, and that wasn't fair to you." Getting comfortable on my lap, she put her arms around my neck. "This is the first time Steven and I have had to navigate someone else who's involved with Grant, too. I think we're all just fumbling about."

"Steven has never introduced any of his girlfriends to Grant?"

"Grant has met a couple, but only because they accidentally showed up at Steven's, not realizing Grant was there. Or there've been a couple of times he's run into one of them while he and Grant were out and about," she explained. "Steven hasn't cared about someone strongly enough yet to introduce them to his son."

I nodded as I realized I had a lot to learn about being a parent and stepparent, because that's where this was going. Of course, I didn't tell Andie this because I wasn't sure if she was still on her take-it-slow kick, but that's where this was definitely headed.

I tightened my hold on Andie's hips. "I need to be honest with you, Andrea," I told her, and she immediately looked wary.

"Uh, okay…"

"I'm going to fuck up again," I blurted. "I'm a super work in progress, and that being said, you're in for the fight of your life if you think I'm going to just let you break up with me every time I screw up. So, think about that and just save us the aggravation, okay?"

She chuckled. "Oh, really?"

I nodded. "We can fight. We can yell. We can silent treatment. We can do all that. But we can't break up. That's non-negotiable." She opened her mouth to argue, I was sure, before I added, "And we can only fight Thursday evening through Sunday evening during the summer, and Friday evening through Sunday evening during the school year."

Her smile lit up her face. "Of course," she agreed.

CHAPTER 25

Andrea ~

This was about as perfect as it got.

Well, almost.

We had a lot to work out, and I knew there was going to be more bumps in the road, but I was all in for this.

I didn't want to be afraid.

And Nathan's love for Grant was clear. There was no way to deny that he adored my son, and that mattered on a big scale.

"I have another confession to make," he blurted again.

"Oh, yeah?"

"I'm in love with you and I have to put that out there because I'm not sure I can contain it," he confessed, and my stomach dipped. "It's going to just come flying out of my mouth, I'm sure, and I don't want to hide it, even if it doesn't go hand-in-hand with your going-slow program." His blues searched mine. "I love you, Andrea," he said. "I love you so much, baby."

"Nathan…"

"I don't need you to say it back," he quickly added. "Especially, if you don't feel it. But I just needed you to know how I felt." He pulled me up higher on his lap. "I'm in this for real."

I knew I was probably already in love with him, but I needed to take this slow for me. I'd only ever said those words to one another man and I didn't take that phrase lightly. It wasn't about being afraid, so much as it was about being sure. So, instead of trying to explain how I felt, I decided to show him.

I leaned in, and as soon as Nathan gauged that I was about to kiss him, his hands darted into my hair and he held me firm as his lips landed on mine. My hands tightened around his neck as I deepened the kiss and hoped he could feel what he did to me.

"Fuck, baby," he rasped out. "Even one day is too long to be without you." I knew exactly what he meant.

"Prove it," I demanded. I knew what Nathan was capable of in bed and I knew my demand would be met with the same determination as he played baseball.

Before I knew it, Nathan had me off his lap and on my knees, facing the back of the couch. I braced my hands on the top of the backrest, and I was already panting with anticipation. My fingers curled into the upholstered wood as Nathan's hands grabbed the waistband of my yoga pants. Being a Saturday morning without my son, I had been lazing around in an old washed-out Hoyas t-shirt and a pair of black yoga pants. My flip-flops had easily come off when Nathan had positioned me where he wanted me.

"I'm going to fuck you so hard, Andrea," Nathan promised against the bare skin of my left hip. "I'm going to bottom out in that sweet pussy of yours."

I moaned and prayed to God he would. "Yes..." I shamelessly begged.

"Yeah?" he rasped out, and I was going to beg some more, but then I realized what he was doing. Nathan had trapped my legs by pulling my pants down only to the bottom of my thighs. I was going to be at his mercy, and the thought was exhilarating.

Nathan grabbed my hips and popped my ass out until my back was arched and I was presented to him for that taking. My fingers were wearing on the backrest and I could feel myself practically dripping with need.

"Fuck, I love the way you smell," he said, right before his large hands grabbed hold of each of my ass cheeks and pulled them apart. "But I love the way you taste even more."

"Oh, God..." I moaned as I felt Nathan's tongue run a long, smooth path from my clit to my ass. My head dropped as Nathan worked his tongued expertly over my sex. I already knew he was particularly skilled at eating pussy, but I planned to never take his talents for granted. "Nathan..."

He pulled away and I felt his thumb rubbing everything within its reach. "Let me get this condom on, baby, and I'll give you exactly what you need." I was so desperate, it was on the tip of my tongue to tell him to forget the condom, but then I remembered he used to be a professional athlete. While I trusted that Nate wouldn't do anything to harm me, a person could never be too safe.

And as if he could read my mind, he said, "After this weekend, we're both getting tested, so I can stop using these fucking things with you. But fair warning, I've never had sex without a condom before, so I'm probably only going to last three seconds the first time." I let out a muffled laugh. "But we'll just have to keep fucking until I build up a respectable tolerance for that tight cunt of yours, baby."

His hands retuned to my ass, and spreading me wide again, I felt his spit land on the rosette of my ass and drizzle downward to mix with the wetness already leaking out of my body.

"Hang the fuck on," he growled, right before he slammed his entire length inside my body.

"*Oh, God...*"

With one hand digging into my hip, I felt the other grabbed a fistful of my hair as Nathan yanked my head backwards. His lips next to my ear, he said, "I can't wait to fuck you raw, Andrea. I can't wait to see my cum leaking out of your body. I can't wait to flood your cunt." My body contracted around him, and he let out a dark chuckle. "You like that? You like thinking about how I'm going to unload inside you?"

"Yes," I moaned, eager for what he was promising.

His thrusts became harder and deeper, and his length was making it almost too painful to take. Nathan's size was always going to be a challenge, but I welcomed it.

Letting go of my hair, both his hands were now digging into my hips as he crashed his body into mine over, and over, and over again. With my legs being held prisoner by my pants, I couldn't even adjust my legs to ease any of the force of his thrusts, and with every stab into my body, Nathan was giving me every inch of his cock. My ass hit his groin with every single drive.

"I'll never get enough of this pussy, baby," he grunted behind me. "It'll never be enough."

"Nathan..."

"Yeah, baby?"

"Please..." I wanted to cum. I *needed* to cum. "More..."

"Fuck, I love the way you beg for my cock," he groaned, and before I could beg for more, I felt another dribble of spit land on my ass. We hadn't gotten around to anal sex yet, but I knew it would only be a matter of time. That thought was confirmed when I felt Nathan's thumb pop past my puckered ring of resistance.

And. I. Moaned.

He started working his thumb in opposite rhythm of his dick and the double penetration had me dripping. "You like that, Andrea? You like me inside your ass?"

"Oh, God...Nathan...oh...oh, God..." I panted.

"Good," he growled. "Because you better believe I'm going to work my cock inside this tight ass of yours soon." My fingers turned white with the grip I had on the couch and I let out choked cry. "That's it, baby. Cum on my cock. Cum on that thick dick while you take my finger up your ass."

Holy fuck.

"*Nathan!*" I threw my head back, and almost broke all my nails on the couch as I came all over him.

"Fuck," he hissed. "Fuck, fuck, fuck...baby..."

"Oh, God..."

"I'm cumming," he warned me. "Keep squeezing my cock, baby."

Whatever else he might be saying was lost in a haze of tremors or was being drowned out by the rush of blood in my ears. My entire body lost its skeletal support, and my head was resting on the backrest of the couch and my body went limp. The only proof of life was my harsh breathing and the twitches of aftermath.

"Jesus Christ," Nathan swore behind me before pulling out of my body. The second he was clear, I collapsed on the couch. Nathan chucked, but I just laid there. My eyes closed, I felt him pulling up my yoga pants, and then I felt a soft kiss on the side of my head.

I wasn't sure if I had passed out or not, but the next thing I knew, Nathan was picking me up and walking us to his bedroom. He laid me down on the bed where he immediately went to work on undressing me, and I let him.

"I take it this is how we're going to spend our Saturday?" I asked lazily.

The gorgeous jerk smirked. "I'll let you eat and get something to drink throughout the day."

Then I broke the news to him as he slid into bed with me. "I have to work today, Nate."

One of his large hands was already cradling one of my naked breasts. "Writing or editing?"

"Editing," I replied, and I loved how he had paid attention to how I did both.

"Fine," he said. "I'll make you a deal." His lips were already skimming my naked shoulder. "Every fifth chapter, you'll take a break, so I can make you cum."

I closed my eyes and moaned as his lips found their way to my nipple. "Sounds like a great idea."

"I thought it might," he chuckled.

EPILOGUE

Nathan ~

This was about as perfect as it got.

Well, almost.

"I still can't believe you prefer football to this," I grumbled at the *still* misguided kid next to me.

"And hockey," he immediately replied. "Don't forget hockey." And the little traitor lifted his hand up over his head to fist bump Gideon as he walked behind Grant's seat.

And Gideon, the asshole, fist bumped him.

"How can baseball still be third?" I asked incredulously. "I mean look around you." Currently we were sitting in one of the VIP player's boxes watching the Condors playing in their first playoff series, and everyone was here. It had taken some planning, but the games fell on Sayer's off rotation, so he was here with Monroe, Leta, and their friends The Merrills. Gideon was here by his grumpy self, while Mom and Dad couldn't make it because they had already scheduled an anniversary get-a-way for this weekend, and their quality time together was more important to them than any of us kids. It was sweet but kind of icky when you thought about your parents like that.

And besides me, Grant, Andie, and Steven in attendance, we had also invited Charlie and Rachel and their kids. The box was packed, and everyone was having a good time. But the kid still favored football and hockey, and it still broke my heart.

"It's because I'm loyal," Grant replied, and I grunted.

I looked over at Andie and she was trying to keep from laughing at me. "It's not funny," I told her.

"It's a little bit funny," she replied.

I wisely kept my mouth shut, but sooner or later, I was going to convince Grant to see the light, and then we'll see who's laughing.

"Our kids are going to like baseball first, just so you know," I informed her.

She looked over at me. "What kids? Whose kids?"

I could hear Steven laugh on the other side of Grant and that was about all that I could take. I stood up, grabbed Andie by her arms, and said, "We need to talk." I glance around the room, and even though everyone was paying attention to the game, I still called out, "We'll be right back." And I swear I could hear Grant's and Steven's laughs trailing behind us.

We exited the box and stood just outside the door when I looked down at the woman that I knew I was going to spend the rest of my life with. *"Our* kids," I clarified.

Her brows shot up. "We haven't even been dating six months, Nate," she so rudely pointed out.

"And?"

She cocked her head at me like I was a lunatic.

"Here's the plan," I told her. "We get engaged at six months, married at the year mark, get pregnant on our wedding night, and pop the kid out all before Grant turns ten, so that he's old enough to help out but not too old not to be interested in his baby brother or sister." Her eyes widened. *"And* that kid, and all the others afterwards, are going to like baseball."

Her eyes darkened. "And if…what if Grant's condition is genetic? What if our kids end up with the same condition?"

I couldn't tell her the truth because I had promised to stay in my lane and respect that Grant had great parents and didn't really need me for the major decision, but as soon as my lane merged with Andie's, I planned on using all that excessive money I had on getting Grant the best specialists in the world. I was going to do everything I could to make his life as limitless as possible. But that was further down the line for when Andie and Steven trusted me with Grant as much as I trusted them.

"Then they can play golf, or…chess, or whatever," I said. "But they'll *like* baseball first."

Her eyes glossed over. "I love you Nathan Hayes," she said simply, but it was everything.

"Not half as much as I love you," I groaned, having finally heard those words from her. "You have no idea, baby."

She grinned. "I have somewhat of an idea." I laughed.

She didn't. She had no idea.

"Let's get back to the game, yeah?" She nodded, and it really didn't get more perfect than this.

The End.

PLAYLIST

Nothing to Hide – Poco
Falls on Me – Fuel
Whatever It Takes – Lifehouse
Smooth – Santana ft. Rob Thomas
The Scientist – Coldplay
Take A Bow – Rihanna
Call It Love – Poco
The Fighter – Keith Urban ft. Carrie Underwood
Good Is Good – Sheryl Crow
What Does It Take – Honeymoon Suite

ABOUT THE AUTHOR

M.E. Clayton works full-time and writes as a hobby. She is an avid reader and, with much self-doubt, but more positive feedback and encouragement from her friends and family, she took a chance at writing, and the Seven Deadly Sins Series was born. Writing is a hobby she is now very passionate about. When she's not working, writing, or reading, she is spending time with her family or friends. If you care to learn more, you can read about her by visiting the following:

Smashwords Interview

Bookbub Author Page

Goodreads Author Page

OTHER BOOKS

The Seven Deadly Sins Series *(In Order)*
Catching Avery (Avery & Nicholas)
Chasing Quinn (Quinn & Chase)
Claiming Isabella (Isabella & Julian)
Conquering Kam (Kamala & Kane)
Capturing Happiness

The Enemy Duet *(In Order)*
In Enemy Territory (Fiona & Damien)
On Enemy Ground (Victoria & William)

The Enemy Series *(In Order)*
Facing the Enemy (Ramsey & Emerson)
Engaging the Enemy (Roselyn & Liam)
Battling the Enemy (Deke & Delaney)
Provoking the Enemy (Ava & Ace)
Loving the Enemy
Resurrecting the Enemy (Ramsey Jr. & Lake)

The Buchanan Brothers Series *(In Order)*
If You Could Only See (Mason & Shane)
If You Could Only Imagine (Aiden & Denise)
If You Could Only Feel (Gabriel & Justice)
If You Could Only Believe (Michael & Sophia)
If You Could Only Dream

The How To: Modern-Day Woman's Guide Series *(In Order)*
How to Stay Out of Prison (Lyrical & Nixon)
How to Keep Your Job (Alice & Lincoln)
How to Maintain Your Sanity (Rena & Jackson)

The Holy Trinity Series *(In Order)*
The Holy Ghost (Phoenix & Francesca)
The Son (Ciro & Roberta)
The Father (Luca & Remy)
The Redemption (Nico & Mia)
The Vatican (Francisco Phoenix Benetti & Luca Saveria Fiore)

The Blackstone Prep Academy Duet *(In Order)*
Reflections (Grace & Styx)

Mirrors (London & Sterling)

The Eastwood Series *(In Order)*
Samson (Samson & Mackenzie)
Ford (Ford & Amelia)
Raiden (Raiden & Charlie)
Duke (Duke & Willow)
Alistair (Alistair & Rory)

The Problem Series *(In Order)*
The Problem with Fire (Sayer & Monroe)
The Problem with Sports (Nathan & Andrea)
The Problem with Dating (Gideon & Echo)

The Pieces Series *(In Order)*
Our Broken Pieces (Mystic & Gage)
Our Cracked Pieces (Rowan & Lorcan)
Our Shattered Pieces (Molly & Grayson)

The Holy Trinity Duet *(In Order)*
The Bishop (Leonardo & Sienna)
The Cardinal (Salvatore & Blake)

The Holy Trinity Next Generation Series *(In Order)*
Vincent & Cira (Vincent Fiore & Cira Benetti)
Salvatore Jr. & Camilla (Salvatore Benetti Jr. & Camilla Mancini)
Emilio & Bianca (Emilio Benetti & Bianca Mancini)
Angelo & Georgia (Angelo Benetti & Georgia Mancini)
Dante & Malia (Dante Fiore & Malia Benetti)
Mattia & Remo (Mattia Mancini & Remo Vitale)

The Rýkr Duet *(In Order)*
Avalon (Avalon & Griffin)
Neve (Neve & Easton)

Standalone
Unintentional
Purgatory, Inc.
My Big, Huge Mistake
An Unexpected Life
The Heavier the Chains…
Real Shadows
You Again
Merry Christmas To Me

Dealing with the Devil

Printed in Great Britain
by Amazon

59462970R00068